Ocher's Dawn

Ocher Jones Western Series
Book One

Mike Gipson

Front Cover Photo – James C. (Charles) Fox
Back Cover Photo – Gayle Gipson
Publisher – M.S. Gipson/Createspace

ISBN-978-1-7321626-0-0

To Gayle

You are my North Star

Acknowledgements

I have been truly blessed by the people that have crossed my path. Each and every one of you has added to this endeavor. There are just too many to name. Thanks to all of you.

To the ladies of the writing group who have endured my attempts, supported me, scolded me and provided insights I neglected - Anne Armezzani, Judy DeCarlo, Lourdes Schaffroth, Janet Schwick and Ann Vitale. Thank you.

Two special people, who pushed, pulled, cajoled, criticized, encouraged and took the time to provide the needed polish for this project:

Anne Armezzani
Jim Brouwer

Kacey – You're never too old to chase a dream.

I wish Mom, Dad and Shawn could have read this.

The End

"We call that ocher, not quite orange and not red," the unseen deckhand said to the young man standing at the starboard rail watching the sunrise. "My people use that color for times of celebration. Red, like that of the fire burning astern of us, is used during our death songs." When the young man turned to thank the seaman, the deck was empty.

Chapter One

"Mr. Rat, tomorrow you will have to feed yourself. As we have discussed, tonight is the night of death," the assassin tells his small companion.

For the last twenty-one days, the assassin has spent the nights concealed in the rice patties observing the routine of the compound below. From the first night a large wharf rat follows the assassin to each observation point. As a friendship grows, the assassin always brings the rat a piece of bread or cheese. The two discuss the plan to assassinate the war lord in the compound below.

"My friend, I regret that you will not have final say in my new name. We have both come to hate the name Little Orphan given to me by the Tong. We have debated this for many hours. One day I will reach a decision but not this night."

The assassin shares his last morsel of cheese, "Mr. Rat, you have been very helpful by pointing out the flaws in my plan. You may wish to go home now. As you know there will soon be a great fire and many people running about. Go, take care of your family." The rat seems to understand, turns and heads away from the black-clad man.

The assassin takes a breath and exhales, slowly refocusing his attention to the task ahead. He is confident of his abilities but reviews the plans he has discussed with the rat.

Observe, attack, defend, and escape is the philosophy of a successful assassin.

Being a merchant, the lowest class of the Japanese Feudal hierarchy, allows the just under six-foot, blond-haired, blue-eyed businessman to move about without challenge. There have been several *chance* meetings in the village market place. The arrogance of the Daimyos, feudal war lord, his target, apparently considers the young businessman nothing more than a cockroach. The days are spent buying trinkets and fending off the street vendors cries of *tabemono*, need food? Followed by *oishii*, tasty. More importantly he is being ignored by the upper classes.

Each evening before retiring to his private sleeping room he establishes a pattern of bowing to the owner of the establishment, *mata ashita*, see you in the morning. *Oyasuminasai,* it is time for sleep, good night. Just in case someone questions his habits. The days and nights have been productive. He now has knowledge of the movements of the sentries, bodyguards, villagers as well as the strength and weakness of each group.

In addition to buying trade goods, the assassin purchases additional clothing for disguises, scented soap to wash away the remnants of the honey pot smell of the rice patties and morsels of food for his friend, Mr. Rat. Each night he sneaks from his room at the waterfront then changes into the peasant clothing to watch the compound below, planning each step to fulfill the assignment. The routine is completed by bathing in the stream, hanging the clothing in the brush to dry and sneaking back to his room.

The Daimyos employs three rings of security for his compound. The first ring patrols outside the walls. The second ring is a foot patrol on the interior of the walls. These two rings consist of untrained local peasants. As is custom, the Shogun has allowed the Daimyos to contract three Samurai bodyguards for personal protection and to guard the Shogun holdings being managed by the Daimyos. The three "highly skilled" Samurai are Samurai in name only. They would be more productive by engaging in origami or bonsai.

Breaching the outer layer of sentries is the first step. The assassin starts a fire well away from his intended point of entrée. The outer ring of guards respond as expected, leaving their posts, rushing to the fire and leaving the perimeter unguarded. Only one guard thinks to ring the alarm bell while the others watch the fire. The interior guards are no better. They stay in position and watch the fire spread. From the adjacent village additional alarms are sounded, panic is beginning to gain momentum.

Watching the fire has destroyed the night vision of all of the guards allowing the assassin to slip into the domain of the war lord's three Samurai. All three must be eliminated along with the war lord. Leave no witnesses. If any of the four is left alive, the honor of the Shogun, the Daimyos and the Samurai requires retribution. For total success the assassin must appear to die by the skill of the Samurai, maintaining honor for all of the hierarchy.

From his vantage point atop the wall he can see the villagers running toward the compound carrying buckets. Their screaming and shouting only add to the panic that continues to grow, along with the fire. The black clad assassin waits on the wall for the two off-duty Samurai to respond as they were trained to do. Protect the war lord.

The highest ranking bodyguard is awakened by the alarm bell and the shouts of the guards and villagers. He can see the fire through the *fusuma*, rice paper door, of his quarters. The three Samurai have trained for all emergencies and he is confident that the planning and skills of he and his warriors can easily protect his employer. *It's only a fire*. As he reaches to slide back the *fusuma*, a small hiss sounds as the rice paper rips. He realizes that he has failed his oath as a Samurai when he sees the arrow protruding from his chest. In a last effort to redeem himself he tries to alert his two companions that the fire is a distraction but the pain of death overwhelms him.

The villagers will deal with the fire as is the plan. The second Samurai knows his primary responsibility is to protect his employer. Under normal circumstances he would navigate through his room in the servant's spaces to the *honden*, main structure, to assist the most junior Samurai on watch. Instead he runs through the smoke and confusion across the compound to the formal entrance to the *honden*. Two black lacquered posts carved with the Shogun's name and titles mark the entrance for guests and dignitaries.

The bodyguard would normally not be allowed to enter the residence through the formal gate but it's the quickest route to his charge. With his back to the fire there's no reflection from the walls. He does not see the piano wire stretched across the entrée way. His momentum carries his headless body through the entrée way onto the greeting space. His head falls onto the teak porch. His eyes show no pain.

The assassin patiently watches the tsunami of fire move toward the barn.

The urgent voices of the peasants and the screams of the horses fill the night.

He hopes Mr. Rat is safe.

The junior Samurai can't wait for his companions to respond. He too concludes that the fire is a diversion.

The war lord screams *oira toubou iza,* we escape now, *kyoukan,* assassin.

The Samurai is not panicked by the circumstances, he is after all a Samurai. They have planned for this possibility. In the stable there are always four horses saddled with provisions for escape. The last bodyguard rushes the war lord toward the stables.

The fire seems to be predatory and turns toward the last remaining prey, the stables and the horses.

The black-clad assassin enters the barn from the small servant's entrance after observing the panicked Samurai and Daimyos abandon the *honden* to rush to the stables. With all of the reverence that can be observed, the assassin recovers the dead body of the old man discovered on the wharf. He dresses the body in his own black garb and puts on the clothes of a peasant.

"Thank you, grandfather," are the only words the assassin can think of. The heat and the fire are becoming overwhelming as the peasant heads toward the stables' double doors.

Suddenly the stable doors are swung wide by the Samurai. All twenty of the estates horses are stampeding directly at the two men. The horses are terrified of the fire behind them and confused by the men in front. The width of the door creates a choke point. The front stampeding horses manage to avoid the two men but not those running full speed in terror at the back of the herd. The contract is complete. The war lord and his bodyguards are dead. Now Little Orphan the assassin must die.

Even before the man dressed as a peasant walks from the barn, the fire reaches the roof timbers. The peasant assists in dragging the bodies of the war lord and bodyguard away from the barn. In the process, he removes the silk sack of jewels from the trampled body of the Daimyos.

The peasant thinks *At least Tong won't get these.*

Chapter Two

*K*asai, *kasai*, Fire, fire the peasant yells, adding to the panic and confusion. He watches the conflagration consume the barn to make certain that the collapse is imminent. *Rukka, kyoukan*, look assassin, he points as the rafters succumb to the inferno. The cry is taken up by those fighting the fire *kyoukan*. Those present will later confirm that an assassin has died in the fire.

The peasant assists in the firefighting effort by carrying empty buckets back to the stream. He makes only one trip. He slips off into the darkness, walks the mile or so through the paths in the rice patties to the small stream. The peasant clothes are buried. He scrubs, using scented soap, hoping to mask the smell of smoke. The clothes he puts on are slightly too big and with just enough wear to reflect a man of limited means traveling abroad on business. The ill-fitting clothes disguise the bulge of the cloth belt where he has hidden the stolen jewels. Before making his way to the wharf where a longboat awaits his arrival he turns, "Goodbye, Mr. Rat, and to you Little Orphan."

The sailing vessel *Anna Belle* certainly does not reflect her genteel name. A shipyard refit that has maximized the cargo spaces makes the ship appear cumbersome. A three-masted Jackass Bark, heavy in the stern and broad at the beam, she seems to wallow just sitting at anchor. Captain Quarte reluctantly agrees to a passenger. The gift of a small gold bell finally helps make the decision. The Second Mate is moved to the crew's quarters making space for the lone passenger. When the traveling arrangements are completed, two small trunks are taken aboard and stowed in the state room.

The longboat is brought aboard and the *Anna Belle* sails on the tide. The young traveler does not go below but stays on deck to watch the crew make sail. The preparations always appear to be chaotic. Weighing the anchor, setting the sheets, stowing mooring lines and making the ship ready for sea are all in a specific order, all this preparation accomplished in the gloom of dark with no moon. The only ambient light is the fire burning on shore. The chain of command is defined: Captain to the sail master to the bosun's mate with the men on and above decks anticipating getting underway. There's no time to talk to the passenger on deck.

The noise aloft is akin to the communication of whistles, barks, and cries of the monkeys and birds in the jungle canopy where he was orphaned. He knows and understands these jungle sounds. The communication of the men in the rigging is with words that have meaning known only to men of the sea. The chatter of the jungle animal is far more comforting than the babble drifting down from the ship's canopy.

Free of the harbor and free from the past, the traveler looks toward the bow feeling the ship take the wind. If the ancient sailors rhyme is correct, (*Red sky at night, sailors' delight. Red sky at morning sailors take warning*) once the sails are set they would need minimum attention during the day watches. The sails are set. The ship sails east away from foul weather, toward San Francisco.

"We call that Shiilooshe, not quite orange and not red," the unseen deckhand says to the young man standing at the starboard rail watching the sunrise. "My people honor that color in times of celebration. Red, like that of the fire burning astern of us, is used during our death songs." When the young man turns to thank the seaman, the deck is empty.

Chapter Three

Sailing is not for the lazy. There's not a minute that isn't filled with some type of maintenance. Swabbing, mending, polishing, scouring the teak decks, rope work, sewing the sails, standing watch, all are done regardless of the weather. There are two methods of maintaining a ship: one is by leading a ship's crew, the other is by pushing. The *Anna Belle's* Captain understands only to push. To do this, his instrument of choice is the ship's bosun, Gunter.

A man six inches over six feet, with green tinted teeth and the odor of a ship's bilge, the man's solo purpose appears to be intimidation. His size would normally be enough to keep the ship's crew motivated but that's not enough for this man. Gunter's booming voice fills the air all day and night, issuing needless commands. The crew are efficient in their duties, but not to his liking. To embellish the intimidation, the deck bosun carries a leather whip with a twelve-inch handle with a two-foot lash. His use of the whip is indifferent as to right or wrong. He uses it because he likes to use it. Every seaman on deck displays the results of the whip ugly red welts, usually on the neck or face. Through fair and foul weather, the bullying and lashing remain a constant.

On the third morning underway, the traveler decides to take in the morning air along with the ever present seawater coming in over the bow. He has also had enough of the bosun's voice and demeanor and is hoping for an opportunity to confront the man. He has calculated the risks and is willing to take a chance if one appears.

The *Anna Belle* is taking the swells over the bow and pitching fore and aft as the morning watch comes on deck with the bosun bellowing commands from the main deck. The traveler approaches the man from astern just as an opportunity appears. The ship's bow drops into a trough between swells as the bosun starts to administer a lash to a deck hand. The traveler uses the momentum of the ship and slides forward into the bosun. The motion of the landlubber surprises the bosun, knocking him slightly off balance.

"Still don't have my sea legs," the traveler says.

Gunter's instinct is to reach out for the hand rail, leaving the whip dangling loose on his wrist. The timing is perfect. The ship regains her momentum shouldering up the next swell. The bow rises, keeping the bosun off balance and pinned against the young man. With what looks like an attempt to steady the bosun by grabbing his arm instead, becomes one swift motion removing the whip from the big man's wrist and dropping it to the deck. The seawater washing down the deck sweeps the whip over the side through a scupper before anyone can react. The duty helmsman sees the whole scene and allows himself a slight smile that crinkles the red whelp on his cheek, the blue-eyed side.

The seas remain unsettled for the next three days allowing the traveler to read, rest, and contemplate such matters as *what is a cowboy*? He takes his meager meals of bread, hardtack, and tea in his cabin. He ventures out occasionally and is surprised by the "tip of the cap" motion from the crewmen when they pass him. On the other ships he has sailed with, that salute is meant for the ship's officers. He also notes that the bosun, a whip no longer dangling from his wrist, has increased his verbal assaults on the crew.

After a week the seas have calmed into long lazy combers, allowing the young traveler to take in some fresh air without getting soaked to the knees from the waves breaking over the bow. Just before he steps onto the main deck, he encounters the unmistakable odor of the ship's bosun. He knows that the big man has been watching the cabin, waiting for the chance to ransack the passenger's meager quarters.

The traveler steps through his cabin door and into the glare of the ship's bosun. The big man smiles thinking he has the advantage in the confined space. "Well, sir, it'll be a real shame that we'll be losing a passenger on this here voyage. The men have grown kind of fond of you." He steps forward with the apparent intent of choking the passenger with his massive hands.

Instead of stepping away from Gunter, the traveler steps forward. The bosun's eyes widen. He is confused. No man has ever stepped into his challenge. Unaccustomed as he is, he starts to back away.

"I wouldn't. That knife you feel under your chin might slip, making a mess in my cabin." To emphasis the effect, the assassin pushes the blade upward, drawing a few small drops of blood.

The big man is now standing on his tip toes, holding his breath, and awaiting instructions.

The assassin retracts the blade and with a quick downward motion slices the lanyard holding up the big man's pants. Gunter reaches for his trousers.

With a dismissive chuckle, the assassin directs, "Don't. Just turn slowly and get out."

From the sounds coming from the passageway, Gunter apparently is unsuccessful in raising his trousers before attempting to flee. When the cursing from outside the cabin door subsides, the traveler decides to continue his walk on deck. Navigating around the drops of blood he steps onto the main deck. He motions to the Deck Officer that he's out and about and receives a slight nod. There are several deck hands sitting on the forward hatch cover. One seaman is teaching fancy rope work and the rest are watching. With his sea legs now under him the traveler proceeds forward. As he approaches, they break up and scatter about the main deck. All but one.

"Evening, Sir," the weathered man with odd eyes says as he makes a motion of tipping his cap. It is the same voice of the seaman who spoke on the first night.

"Evening," comes the reply. "I didn't mean to intrude on the crew."

"No bother, sir. They just don't know what to make of you. They saw the bosun go forward bleeding a bit and trying to keep his pants aloft. What a pity."

The passenger makes small talk about the weather, food, and Ports of Call. After a bit he asks, "Being a sailor seems to be a tough life. Do you enjoy it?"

"No disrespect, sir," he says as he slides closer to the traveler. In a whisper, "I am not a sailor. I was Shanghaied two years back and stayed aboard so I could get back home to America."

"You are from America?" the traveler interrupts the seaman. "Sorry, I'm just surprised.

"Aye, sir. There are several of us aboard that are trying to get home. I've said too much already. By your leave sir, I'll be going below." He stands, makes fast the rope work, picks up the sail palm, twine and fid. The seaman starts toward the sail locker, stops and turns. "The Captain and the bosun are like a shark and a pilot fish: they rely on each other. Whatever

happened aft just now between you and the
bosun, it was the same as the Captain being
there. You need to stand a tight watch on that
pair."

Now alone on deck, the traveler turns aft to
return to his cabin when the Second Mate
approaches, "The Captain invites you to supper,
six bells."

"Please tell the Captain it will be a pleasure,
six bells."

Chapter Four

Just as the peal of the last of six bells begins to fade, the traveler knocks on the door of the Captain's cabin.

"Enter."

The young man opens the small door and walks into the Captain's stateroom. "Thank you for the invitation, Captain."

The Captain is sitting at the head of a table that is covered with navigation charts, tide tables, sextant and two place settings of dinnerware. He looks up and points to the place setting on the starboard side of the table. "Sit there. The navigator has just given me the evening positions. I have to confirm our course, and supper will be served shortly. The steward will serve you some wine if you like."

The traveler knows that the dinnerware placed among the navigation debris is intended as an insult. His instincts are confirmed when he turns toward the port side of the cabin where the small galley and scullery are located. The steward, a portly, ruddy faced man, is standing just inside the doorway to the galley. He makes a quick gesture of placing his fingers against his lips with a slight shaking of his head.

The young guest notes the gesture. "Just some hot water for tea please. The sea doesn't agree with me. The tea seems to settle my sickness."

The Captain looks up from his calculations. "Pity, this was to be a special meal, just for you." He lays his calipers on the table. "Be warned, young man. You may think you have moral authority to do as you please. On this ship there is only one authority, me. I decide all things. Respect it. We are still a long ways from port, and well," he meets the traveler's eyes with a cold hard stare, "let's just say it's a cold swim to anywhere."

The traveler returns the glare. "Respect is earned, sir, through leadership and knowledge, not by intimidation and fear. When you and that ape have earned it, I'll give it. At least the bosun has the tenacity to do his own dirty work. You on the other hand.... ." The Captain's guest starts toward the cabin door, stops and turns. "One last thing, Captain. Do you know if the bosun can swim? We are, after all, a long way from port and it is a cold swim to anywhere."

Chapter Five

An assassin is trained to observe patterns and to take advantage of them. Each day at exactly two bells, the bosun retires below decks. The exact same time as the traveler comes on deck. The deck hands recognize the pattern and take the opportunity to share scuttlebutt with the traveler. When Gunter reappears on deck the crew set about being busy or at least looking busy. When Gunter and the traveler are on deck together there's always an off-duty seaman, leaving no opportunity for the bosun to catch him alone.

The traveler seems comfortable with one man in particular, the Shanghaied sailor, a half Crow Indian and half Mexican. His name is *Ojos Loco*, Crazy Eyes because of his one blue and one brown eye. Each time the two meet and talk, Ojos shares a little more about his home in the high desert northward into the Canadian Provinces. All he wants is to return to the wilderness where he can control his own destiny, not at sea where he controls nothing.

The color of the sea begins to change from the deep azure blue to the light blue color of the sky. The smells of the sea have changed as well. The aroma of pine trees, soil and sand begin to filter over the *Anna Belle*. Just as the morning watch is relieved, a hail from aloft "Land ho, off the port quarter." The coast of America comes into view.

One of the seasoned sailors turns to the traveler, "I make it out to be half a day north of San Francisco."

The Captain and Gunter make an extraordinary effort to keep the crew so busy that they take no note of the coast line. Instinct and the bosun's glare tell the traveler that there's trouble brewing. He will take additional measures to assure his health and future.

Just as the ship's bell is struck indicating the mid-watch has started, a commotion erupts on deck. The traveler trusts his instincts. He knows his chances of survival are greater on the open deck than in this small confined cabin. Without hesitation he heads on deck. There's nothing of any value here anyway. The stolen jewels are now safely secured in cloth belts around his body and covered by the ill-fitting clothes.

He moves with caution into the passageway. He notes immediately that the seaman that normally sits protecting the stateroom is not present. As he reaches the doorway to the main deck, the voice of the Captain can be heard. "Get those men below and in irons. Chain them in the hawser locker."

Under the full moon the traveler can see that the men being confined are the men who have been protecting him from Gunter. It would appear that as soon as they were relieved from the evening watch, they were to be confined below deck. Without any interference the Captain and bosun can proceed with whatever they have planned. From the confrontation taking place forward the men are resisting being taken below and being chained.

There is a great deal of confusion being orchestrated by the Captain shouting orders. The first officer is forward relaying the orders to the deck hands who are trying to confine their ship mates. The confrontation appears to be out of hand except to the trained observer. The whole scene is a diversion. The traveler sees it for what it is immediately. Two men are missing from the scene, the bosun's mate and Ojos. The traveler takes one step forward and is assaulted by the bosun and his stench.

The big man is waiting in the shadows just below the bridge deck. He steps out to confront the traveler. "I won't make any mistake this time little man," Gunter moves forward as the aggressor.

There will be no escape for the big man. There will be no mercy this time. The assassin stands his ground, feints a move to his right and delivers a roundhouse kick to the outside of bosun's right knee. The tendons and muscles holding the joint in place, give way with a snap. But the big man does not go down. The pain has not registered in his brain so the assassin delivers a roundhouse to the other knee. The pain finally arrives and the bigger man goes down.

"Captain!" The bosun screams.

The Captain turns from the melee on the quarterdeck and looks aft. He sees the bosun writhing on the deck and the passenger standing over him. The Captain pulls a flintlock pistol from his waistband and takes aim. The traveler hears the percussion cap ignite just as Ojos grabs him around the waist and they both go over the starboard rail and into the Pacific Ocean.

Chapter Six

"Don't take a breath," is the traveler's only thought just before impact with the cold Pacific Ocean. Remain calm, let the initial shock of the water pass, swim to the surface, then take a deep, calm breath. His thought process is organized. However, the frigid Pacific Ocean immediately rearranges the plan. Remaining calm seems to have been driven from his mind, replaced by, "Get to the surface and breathe."

As he breaks the surface, the plan is to take deep calm breaths. A gasp for air seems far more appropriate resulting in half air and half water. The next breath is mostly air. The traveler treads water making a complete turn. Ojos is swimming toward him and the *Anna Belle* is sailing away making no apparent attempt to rescue the men.

The seas are calm and the two men are close enough to talk in between breaths. Ojos speaks first. "We were about a league," breathe "off the coast when I came off watch." Breathe, "Just swim into the reflection off the moon on the water." Breathe, "You can swim can't you?"

The traveler responds. "My shoes are going to weigh me down." The effort to remove his shoes is far more difficult than anticipated. The heel to toe method doesn't work, the laces are too tight. He removes his knife, cuts the laces, and reluctantly lets the shoes go.

Ojos treads water watching the traveler froth up the ocean trying to discard the shoes. He hasn't worn shoes since being Shanghaied.

Stroke, stroke, stroke, breathe and repeat, don't let the mind wander, concentrate on the next stroke and the next breath. The men establish a rhythm and stick to it. No conversation. No worry about what may be stalking them, just the next stroke, and the next breath. Stopping only to check that the other is near, they continue the cadence of survival. During one brief respite the traveler can see that the stars have disappeared on the horizon. It takes his mind a moment to interpret what he is seeing. The stars aren't visible because there's something obstructing them, land. No time to revel in their progress, back to the cadence.

A dull grey dawn reveals the coast, no ocher sunrise, just black then grey. The men can see their goal and hear the surf breaking on the beach. Without fanfare or celebration they are washed ashore just like any other piece of flotsam. They crawl above the surf line. They conduct a weary eyed self-examination to account for body parts. They both know standing up is out of the question, because the cold of the ocean has made their legs useless, for now. The traveler turns to Ojos, "Yep, I can swim."

Ojos stands and looks out toward the ocean. Rubbing his legs, he attempts a small step. "I don't believe the good captain is considering a rescue. We should get a fire going to get warm," Ojos says. "You ready to try walking? I'll get the tinder, you gather up some of the drier drift wood."

The traveler stands, "A brisk walk will do me good," and wobbles off down the beach.

They have washed ashore on a cliff-sheltered beach. Each end of the two-mile-long coast line is cut off by an outcrop of collapsed rock from the cliffs. The only way out is up the rock face. At a glance, the rock face appears to be impossible to climb but by the time the first load of wood has been gathered, the traveler has identified a couple of possible escape routes.

The traveler is curious to see how his companion will start the fire. He watches Ojos remove what appears to be an arrowhead from the pouch he wears around his waist. By striking the arrowhead with the blade of his rigger's knife, he creates a spark that lands in the tender. The dry bundle immediately catches fire. The traveler has never used this method, but it does appear easier than the wood spindle he has used in the jungle.

The traveler stakes out two forked pieces of drift wood near the fire. He removes his shirt and pants and drapes them over the arms of the stakes, revealing the cloth sash and his tattoo.

"I have never seen such a marking. Many of the sailors had tattoos but nothing like that," Ojos does not comment on the sash.

"It is the mark of the people who owned me." The traveler decides that he has to trust someone in this land. Ojos is to be trusted.

Ojos is silent while hanging his wet clothes on the wood. "You find us a way out of here?" Ojos asks, as he adds wood to the small fire.

The traveler responds. "South there is a fresh water stream that has eroded the cliff face. I'll tend the fire if you want to go get a drink of fresh water. I think we can climb out there."

Ojos nods, "I could use a drink of water," and starts down the beach.

The warmth of the fire has begun to revive the traveler's spirit when Ojos returns with an armful of wood. "You're right. That does seem to be the only safe way off this beach. Let's get dried out and get started. It will be hours before the sun reaches this beach and I don't want to waste time standing around this fire to stay warm. Once we get into the trees, we can hunt, build some shelter and rest." Ojos looks at the traveler's feet. "It's going to be tough on your feet."

The young man smiles, "I didn't have any shoes until I left the island a year ago. I'll be fine."

Ojos kicks sand onto the fire but, before he starts out, he looks at his companion. "What do I call you?"

The younger man hesitates before responding. "I was called Maliit Ulila in the

Philippine village where I was raised. It means 'little orphan'. I don't care for it."

Ojos doesn't respond immediately. He just stands and finally, with a guttural grunt he seems to reach some decision. "I see that name is heavy on your heart so we will name you as my people have been taught."

"I would like that," the traveler responds.

Ojos continues, "In each new life the ancient ones teach to observe what we recall first. That is what you are called. I saw my reflection in a pool of water. My eyes were different colors so I became Ojos."

"In the village I was an orphan. Now I am here in a new much larger village, America," the traveler says.

Ojos asks, "What did you see on your first day of your new life?"

The traveler looks at Ojos, "The dawn. You called it *Shiilooshe*."

"So it will be. You will be called *Shiilooshe*." The decision having been made, Ojos just nods and starts back down the beach following the fading footprints they had previously made.

Chapter Seven

The sun appears to be at its zenith, local apparent noon, as the men stop at the top of the cliff face and dip out a handful of water. They are both tired but don't stop to rest. They move into the forest. The traveler is so focused on the gigantic trees before him that he walks right into Ojos, who is also gazing at the trees. Both men look into the forest. They can't look up to the tops as they would topple over backward if they tried. Ojos wipes his hand on the back of his neck, "I have heard of this place, but thought it was just a story told by the old ones. Now I will have my own story to tell. Let's find a place for camp, hunt, and rest. Tomorrow we should leave." There is no response, just a nod of the head from the traveler.

In his jungle, Shiilooshe had experienced a drastic change in temperature, humidity and sunlight walking from the beach into the jungle. There is also a dramatic change here, but it's the overwhelming scent of the forest that he smells. The odor of the trees and ground litter is so fragrant and pleasant. The contrast is different from the humidity and odor of rotting vegetation of the jungle.

The change in Ojos is noticeable as well. With each breath his complexion brightens, his eyes shine and the grin on his face grows. He stops and is speaking in a low tone in a language the traveler does not understand. Ojos turns to Shiilooshe, "I have thanked the ancient ones for bringing us to this place and have asked for good hunting as we travel. We go."

Ojos's transformation continues. On the ship he was quiet, pensive, guarding his thoughts and actions. Now he is animated, showing his companion the small animals, birds, flowers, plants and how all things interact. He no longer uses the jargon of the sea. They follow the steam into the forest for several miles when Ojos turns. "We should make camp, start a fire and hunt. I would prefer the hunt." Shiilooshe has been watching the change in Ojos since they started off the beach. He will not deprive Ojos of the hunt. He suspects that the hunt is secondary to the Indian's purpose. The real reason is to walk through the forest that he has missed so much.

Ojos is carving a curved stick with his knife, "This is a throwing stick. Until I can make a bow and arrows, this will have to do." Shiilooshe pulls a rock sling from his pocket and offers it to Ojos. "Will this help?"

Ojos' smile almost breaks his face. "I haven't used one of those since I was a boy. This fills my heart with joy." He accepts the rock sling, takes an arrowhead from the bag at his waist, "This is flint. Strike this with your hidden knife to produce a spark to start a fire," then disappears into the forest without a sound.

When Ojos returns, he looks at the site and smiles. "I have never seen a camp like this before. We have much to learn about each other's way of life. Have you ever seen a bird like this?" He holds out a large, dark feathered bird.

"No." The traveler responds, "We have a similar bird, not as heavy with flat black feathers with small white spots. It is called a guinea fowl. That bird's feathers have shades of black that show as you move it. What is it?"

"This is a turkey. I'll prepare it, and then while we eat, you must explain to me this camp."

Ojos dresses out the bird quickly. He saves all of the long tail feathers explaining he will use them to make arrow fletching. "Why do you build a fire using green wood? As you can see there's much smoke?"

"Mosquitoes," is the reply. "In the jungle there are so many mosquitoes at night, the smoke keeps them away."

"That is wise," Ojos replies. "That's why you have placed the sleeping area down wind, so the smoke will cover you while you sleep."

"Yes."

"See that tree over there, the one with the peeling bark. If you take the leaves, rub them between your hands that will make oil. Rub the oil on your skin and the mosquitoes will not come to you. White men call that Eucalyptus."

Ojos removes the green wood, setting it aside, and replaces it with dry wood.

Shiilooshe walks to the Eucalyptus tree removes some of the leaves and makes the oil as Ojos has suggested, "This is much easier than enduring the smoke."

"I see you used vines and poles to build a platform for sleeping. Why did you build these beds above the ground with a cover over them?"

Shiilooshe recognizes immediately that he has become a teacher, but also a student. He is being taught new ways to survive but at the time teaching the same. "The jungle has many predators, some from the ground some from above. The raised platform keeps ants, scorpions, spiders and smaller snakes from joining you during sleep. The ground predators hunt other animals on the ground. The covering keeps off the rain, bird droppings, and large snakes. It also stops the monkeys from throwing debris at you."

Ojos smiles, "I have seen these monkeys. They are annoying. You have been taught well. I also see you have considered escape routes. Your camp is good. You have been taught well for your jungle."

"Ojos, my friend, I have much to learn about this land. If my ways are not good, tell me."

"In your jungle you have many dangers and your ways are good for those dangers. Here there're only three predators. Bears and mountain cats don't like the smell of man and will not come into our camp."

Shiilooshe has many questions but sits silently waiting for Ojos to continue.

"Man is the hunter that's to be avoided. The smoke of the fire will tell him where you are. The lazy ones will come for whatever you have. It's wiser to have a fire with no smoke or no fire at all. I don't think we are followed, but there could be others already in this place." He reaches for the green boughs he has taken from the fire, strips the green foliage. Then weaves the branches around the turkey and suspends the bird basket over the embers on upright sticks he has driven into the ground. Supper begins to cook.

While the bird cooks over the smokeless fire Ojos continues teaching the traveler about the sounds of his forest especially how to recognize the different warnings of the crickets, frogs, and night birds.

With full stomachs and crickets standing watch, the men climb onto the sleeping platforms and are immediately engulfed in their exhaustion.

It's not the sun that wakes the traveler but the change of sounds in the surrounding forest. The soft voices of the night birds transition to the raucous celebration of the morning birds. The crickets and frogs have been relieved of the watch by the squirrels. A soft breeze has displaced the stillness of the night.

Ojos has revived the fire and retrieved the remnants of the turkey that he had hung from a limb away from camp. "Bears don't like the smell of man, but they do like turkey," had been the last lesson the night before.

"My friend," Ojos says as he points to the area around the campsite. "As I have said, your camp is good for the jungle, but we can't hide it so easy. Look, see where you have cut the branches for the sleeping platforms. The ends are white. The smell of smoke is in the trees and the rocks for the fire pit have been moved and are black. We must learn from this. Leave no trace for those who might follow."

The traveler is not offended by the remark. He recognizes the value of the lesson and more importantly he recognizes the value of the teacher.

The camp is broken down and their presence erased as best as it can be. To a casual observer there's no trace of the overnight stop. But to the trained eye the site stands out in the forest like a beacon. Another lesson learned.

The trek eastward takes all day. Ojos teaches what the forest offers. Plants that can be eaten and what should be avoided. The blueberries, blackberries, thistle, and pine nuts are gathered and eaten. The shiny leaves of the poison oak are avoided. At approximately noon, the men stop beside a small meandering stream that has a shallow pool in the shade of a willow tree. While soaking his bare feet in the ankle deep pool, the traveler sees several small fish swimming. "Want some fresh fish?"

Ojos looks up from peeling open a large pine cone. "Yes. I will start a fire, if you can catch one."

The traveler picks up a large flat rock, moves slowly into the crystal clear water, stops, raises the stone then hesitates. Stepping out of the stream he turns to Ojos. "Slamming a flat rock into the water will stun the fish. We can take what we need and in a minute the rest will swim away. It also makes much noise. I have a better way."

Ojos smiles, "You are learning Shiilooshe."

The assassin wades back into the knee high stream. He moves slowly to a shaded area close to the bank. He bends forward and strikes.

Ojos hears the flopping of a fish behind him. He turns just in time to see his traveling companion reach into the water with the speed of a snake and catch a second fish barehanded.

"Is two enough?"

Ojos has caught fish by using his hands to cradle the fish then raising them out of the water. He has never seen anyone that could do what Shiilooshe has just done. "Two is enough, now you must clean them."

With lunch cooking, Ojos says, "I must return to my people soon. The leaves are falling from the trees and the snows will come soon to my home. Do you still travel to San Francisco?"

The traveler smiles at Ojos, "Yes, I wish to thank the good captain for making the effort to rescue us. After that, I do not know. There is much to learn in this America. I know you could teach me much more, but your heart is with your family."

Ojos looks at the traveler, "I can teach you how to survive in my world, but not the white man's world. I do not wish to be in that world ever again." He hesitates before continuing. "In six new moons be in Salt Lake City. Camp between the two lakes. I will find you."

The traveler stands and offers his hand to Ojos. "Thank you, my friend. Are you sure you can find my camp?"

Ojos smiles at Shiilooshe and shakes the offered hand. "I will try."

Chapter Eight

Slowed by the hilly terrain, the men cover only ten miles.

"Shiilooshe, it would be wise to stop above the road. If we continue, the darkness will make it difficult to make a camp. We will be much safer up there. Tomorrow will be soon enough to go down where the wagons travel."

Shiilooshe nods in agreement.

The camp is set up inside the tree line for protection. The fire is placed in a small hollow so as not to be seen, especially from the road. The sleeping areas are swept clean of pine needles and leaves to avoid ticks. During the day's walk, Ojos using the sling, has killed and dressed two squirrels. Both men are tired but exhilarated at the same time and eager to indulge in the fresh meat roasting over the fire.

South of their camp a plume of smoke is visible. Ojos points, "White men. That is the place where the freight wagon men eat, change mules, buy supplies and sell gold. It is an easier journey to San Francisco for you in a wagon than with bare feet."

"You have been here before?"

"Yes." Ojos stands and walks into the shadows surrounding the camp. He returns with fire wood although none is needed. You are my friend so I will tell you this story one time and then I do not wish to speak of it again."

"I understand."

"I was infected by the white man's words. Three men came to our camp in the high mountains. They had many pouches of gold. They needed a guide to bring them to that place." Ojos says pointing with a stick toward the direction of the chimney smoke. "In return I was to receive a new long gun I thought I needed. When we reached this road, they attacked me, tied me up, placed a cloth in my mouth and covered my head with a burlap sack. Later I was thrown in a wagon and covered up."

Ojos stirs the fire with his stick, "I could smell the mules and the food from the store but could not move or speak. Sometime later, I could not tell how long, I was taken from the wagon. I was struck on the head and woke up on the *Anne Belle* at sea." He pauses and then throws the stick into the fire.

Shiilooshe does not know what to say. He sits quietly listening to the night sounds.

"I am glad to be home and to return to my family."

"How long will it take to get to your village?"

Ojos considers the question. "Three to four weeks on foot."

The traveler reaches into the waist band of his tattered pants, extracts five gold Japanese Yen coins and hands them to Ojos. "Your journey will be easier if you have some supplies and a mule."

Ojos looks at the coins, hesitates and finally accepts them, "Yes, it will be easier." Placing the gold pieces into a pocket, he makes the small grunting sound that the traveler has learned, means that a decision has been made and the conversation has ended.

The pine needles are spread over the sleeping area and the now-dead fire. Ojos takes a pine sprig and sweeps the dirt, erasing any evidence of their camp. They follow a small stream down the slope into the canyon bottom. The sun is well up when the two men reach the road. The ruts in the road tell the tale: this is a freight wagon road.

The men step into the road and start south toward the rising plume of smoke.

"It is said that the wagons transport goods to the gold camps in the north. The returning wagons take lumber and gold back to San Francisco," Ojos says.

The two men can hear the rattle of the trace chains and the grating of steel-rimmed wheels as wagons approach. They step out of the road and onto the edge of the vegetation alongside the road. The sounds grow louder until they can see four mules pulling a loaded wagon, followed by three more wagons. The first team is driven by a slim man sporting a small brimmed hat.

Without warning, the lead wagon's teamster lashes out with a bull whip toward Ojos, "Out of the way breed." The snap of the whip just over their heads is followed by a mouthful of tobacco spit aimed at Ojos as the wagon passes by. The glob hits the ground, raising a small dust plume just short of Ojos' left foot. Before Ojos can stop him, Shiilooshe launches a rock from his sling. The stone catches the driver just above the right ear with sufficient velocity that the small brimmed cloth hat is knocked off his head and onto the ground right into a wagon rut. There's not enough space for the lead wagon to stop so all four wagons run over the hat before they disappear down the road. Shiilooshe walks over, picks up the hat, looks south in the direction of the wagons, saying, "I think I'd like to return this."

Ojos replies, "They will stop at the station, change mules and eat. We can be there before they continue on."

In less than an hour, the traveler and his companion arrive at the change station. There are two buildings: a two-story barn with stable and the store. The barn is surrounded by corrals holding dozens of mules.

"See what the white man does. This place was taken away from the forest and the animals. Instead of the fragrance of the land we smell the manure and burning trash. Just for the yellow metal they destroy the lands," Ojos says.

Shiilooshe nods in agreement. The whole arrangement seems out of place, a two acre barren piece of ground with two buildings right in the middle of the pristine forest. The braying of the mules invades the serene chatter of the animals in the surrounding trees. This combined with smell of the mules is disquieting. Ojos points to a wagon apart from the four that had passed them earlier. The new wagon stands out. There are eight mules in harness while the others have only four. The overall length looks to be twice that of the others and the seat is fortified by what appear to be railroad ties.

The men are drawn toward the rancorous activity of the mules. The mules being removed from their traces don't want to go in the corral and those in the corral don't want to be put in the traces. There's much discussion between man and animal. The outcome is obvious despite the complaints of the braying mules.

"My hat, I'll be taking it," the thin man from the first wagon says walking toward them as he places a cut of tobacco in his mouth. "And then I'll be thanking you proper for this knot on my head."

Shiilooshe looks casually at the teamster, noting that there are three more men standing slightly behind the man. Without hesitation he drops the man's hat into a pile of fresh mule manure, "You owe my friend an apology."

Ojos has seen his companion's unusual skills before. He's curious about how his traveling companion intends to proceed. Will it be with brute force as with Gunter or with finesse as with the fishing? Or could there be some other skill? He leans casually against the wheel of the large wagon, propping one leg up on a spoke. Out of sight of the others he palms his knife, just in case.

The thin teamster eyes widen in disbelief at the location of his hat. He spits in the direction of Shiilooshe, rolls up the sleeves of his red and black checkered shirt. "That is an unkind way to treat a good hat. You can pick it up and clean it now or clean it when I finish with you." The man's intention is to lull the young man with a slow and deliberate approach. He inches forward. With about five feet separating the two men, the wagon driver rushes forward.

Shiilooshe lets him come straight in. When there's one step left between them, he lowers his center of gravity by stepping forward with the left foot then drives the heel of his right hand directly into the middle of the oncoming man's chest. The impact stops the forward motion of the rushing man in mid-stride. The man's legs and arms continue forward, suspending him in space. With his whole body off the ground, gravity takes hold and the man lands flat on his back, swallowing his chaw.

The three on-lookers, friends of the downed man, see no humor in the turn of events and rush the traveler with the intention of overwhelming him with sheer numbers. Ojos, seeing the three men converging on his traveling companion asks, "Need any help?"

"I don't think so."

Shiilooshe focuses his attention to the closest of the three, steps inside of the man's grasp, grabs him around the neck, applying a choke hold. With one combatant now in front of him, he uses the first man as a shield to fend off the blows of the other two attackers. The human shield goes limp and is dropped. Without warning the confrontation stops. Ojos is slack-jawed and gaping at something behind Shiilooshe. The two remaining combatants have also stopped and are focused on whatever Ojos is seeing.

The action has taken the fight up against the mule team of the large wagon. Shiilooshe turns and places his left forearm on the lead mule of the team.

Standing not fifty feet from the group outside of the entrance to the store is the biggest man the traveler has ever seen. Gunter, the ship's bosun of the *Anna Belle* was big, but nothing like this. The giant bends down as he steps into the yard so he doesn't hit his forehead on the half roof covering the porch. His shoulders are wider than Ojos and Shiilooshe's combined width. With what seems like three or four strides, the giant covers the fifty feet to where two men lie on the ground recovering. The teamster's two companions stand perfectly still. Ojos and Shiilooshe just stare.

"I don't like to be disturbed while eating my pie," is the big man's opening statement. "So, who started this? I can see who finished it, you," pointing at the traveler. "What happened?"

"He," the traveler responds pointing with his chin to the man in the checkered shirt, "owes my friend an apology."

One of the two teamsters starts to speak, but the big man cuts him off by holding up a bear sized hand. "You haven't told the truth since I knowed ya, so shut up." He takes one step over to the man in the plaid shirt who is now trying to sit up, and picks him up by the collar of the shirt with the same ease of a cat picking up a kitten. "Apologize."

"But Ollie...." the man starts to say.

"Don't run your yap, besides, look." He points the dangling man toward the traveler leaning on the lead mule of the big wagon. "Honey Bee hasn't bitten him or kicked him. We all know she's a great judge of character."

"Sorry, mister," the man mutters.

"That your hat?"

The dangling man nods. Ollie, still holding the man off the ground, reaches down and picks the cap out of the manure and places it squarely on the man's head, then drops him to the ground. "Get headed south, before I let that kid finish you all off."

With no further discussion, the four men scrabble aboard their wagons and are quickly out of sight.

Chapter Nine

Ollie walks over to the mule trough to wash his hands of any mule debris from the teamster's hat. Wiping his hands on his trousers, "Well, don't you two look a sight. Bet there's a story there? Son, you best be moving away from Honey Bee. She can only tolerate politeness for so long. You're about to wear out your welcome. I'm gonna go finish my pie." He turns, takes a couple of steps and forces his bulk through the door of the station house.

Shiilooshe strokes Honey Bee, "Thanks for letting me rest here a bit," then follows Ojos and the big man toward the station house. The two smaller men enter the door side-by-side, but still don't fill the opening as Ollie had. The aroma of baked goods, coffee, leather, gun oil and soap fill the air in contrast to the mule sweat and manure of the staging area outside. Ollie is indeed having pie, a whole pie.

"Don't just stand there. Sit. How'd you come to be here?" The spoon scrapes the pie dish. "Now where's my manners. Hungry?" Without waiting for an answer, "Dolsey, if I didn't eat it all, could you bring my friends some vittles?"

From the back of the store a woman's voice answers, "I always make extra when I know you're coming. It'll be right out. Won't be no pie. Someone ate it all."

"Where you headed?" he asks between bites of what appears to be apple pie. "I'm headed south to Frisco, soon as I finish my pie and those lazy loafers out in the barn load my wagon."

The traveler waits until Ollie has a mouth full of pie, "We were washed overboard a while back. Found the road and came here. I'm headed south and my friend is headed north."

"Washed overboard were you? I'd bet my best team of mules, not Honey Bee mind you, that you were washed over from the *Anna Belle*."

There's no comment from the two men.

"No answer is good enough. Didn't come looking for you either I bet."

Again no answer.

"Well, ain't headed north, so you're on your own," he says pointing the spoon at Ojos. Moving the spoon in the direction of Shiilooshe, "You can ride along if you have a mind to." The big man pauses getting a breath between bites. Aiming the spoon at Ojos, "Tell you what I can do. I've got two older mules out in the corral, not much good for pulling that big wagon but they'd be a good pack animal, ten dollars for the pair if you want them."

Ojos nods his head, and places a gold Yen on the table. "Thanks."

Ollie stands, avoiding hitting his head on a rafter and picks up the coin. He reaches into his right front pants pocket and pulls out a leather snap coin purse. After rummaging through the coins in the poke he places a ten dollar coin on the table. "You got a name, son?"

"Ojos."

"That about right, Ojos?" he asks pointing toward the ten dollar gold eagle.

"Deal," Ojos says offering his hand to Ollie.

A small woman in a stained gingham dress places two plates full of stew and biscuits on the table. Looking at Ojos, "You're a friend of Ollie's so you're welcome here."

Ollie appears to want to say something to the woman but just wipes his mouth on his canvas cloth shirt, looks at the traveler, "Don't dally over them vittles. We got introductions to make. Bring it if you ain't ate it."

"Yes, sir." Both men respond by picking up their plates of stew and biscuits and follow Ollie out the door.

Ollie is at the corral stroking the graying muzzle of a mule and whispering something into the animal's ear. A second mule is standing patiently next to the first, waiting for the same attention. "Ojos, this is Nell and that other beauty is Bell. Nell is the one with part of her ear missing. There was a bit of misunderstanding between Honey Bee and Nell."

"I will take good care of them," Ojos says offering half a biscuit to Nell and the other half to Bell.

Ollie smiles, "Looks like you're off to a good start."

Ojos turns to Shiilooshe, "Take care, my friend. I shall see you in Salt Lake City in six new moons."

The traveler offers his hand to Ojos, "Does Shiilooshe translate into English?"

"Yes," Ojos places his plate on top of a corral post and takes the offered hand, "It means ocher."

" The old ones have spoken. My new life has dawned, my name will be Ocher."

Ocher responds to Ollie's call, "Let's get on with it." The large wagon is loaded with some type of fur pelts. Two men are just finishing tying down the load. The mules are restless, moving from one leg to the other with an occasional braying complaint.

Ocher finishes shoveling in the stew using a biscuit as a spoon and hurries to the wagon.

Ollie, with a graceful heave, steps into the wagon. The wagon settles with a groan. He moves his bulk to one side of the reinforced seat, looks at Ocher, "Well?"

Ocher hands the empty plate to one of the men who loaded the wagon with a "Thanks," places his bare foot on a wagon spoke, steps up and sits down.

Ollie takes up the reins, taking great care to place each lead in between the fingers of each hand. He adjusts the tension as Ocher has seen violinist tune their violins. When he is satisfied and in a voice just loud enough, "OK, Honey Bee, let's go home." The lead mule steps out, putting a strain on the harness, and the rest of the team responds.

Ocher turns to see Ojos, plate in hand, enter the trading post.

The wagon trail meanders through the hilly terrain keeping Ollie's attention of the trail. He speaks only to the team. When the trail flattens out, Ollie stops at a stream crossing and lets the mules drink. He pulls the team off the trail, "I'll give 'em a breather before we move on. Step down, so I don't have to crowd you none."

Ocher steps down.

Ollie follows him as the wagon creaks in protest, "Sounds like that old wagon is suffering from my sweet wife Marta's good cooking. I'll either have to build a bigger wagon or give up eating."

Ocher smiles at Ollie, "A bigger wagon sounds to be a better choice."

The wagon trail seems to be leading into a grassy open valley surrounded by hill country. Ocher is disappointed at leaving the lush forest and the fresh aroma of the trees. This smells more like farming country, without the aroma of honey pots.

"We've dallied long enough. You ready, Honey Bee?"

The mule stomps one foot and then takes a strain on the trace. "All right, all right." Ollie steps into the wagon amid the now familiar groaning of the wagon, "Yep, bigger wagon."

"Ocher, take a piece of advice. There's gonna be hob to pay when you get to Frisco."

"I have anticipated some."

"Well, son, there's more to it than you know. Since the *Anna Belle* sailed from Frisco two years ago she has been sold to a man of no nonsense. I suspect the whole crew will be set ashore upon arrival."

The wagon lurches, causing Ollie to question Honey Bee's eyesight. "Please, Honey Bee, I know you are yearning for home, but watch where you're going."

The lurch has tossed Ocher to the side. He teeters on the outer edge of wagon seat.

"Easy son, don't want you going over the side again." Ollie grabs Ocher and hauls him back from the precipice.

Ocher resettles in his position, "I can take care of myself, most of the time."

Ollie chuckles at the irony, "I seen that, but Captain Quarte will blame everybody but himself for his problems. Starting with you I suspect. The crew, well some sailed willingly and some not so willingly, and I'm sure none took too kindly to that bosun Gunter. The captain has friends on the waterfront that will hire on to any task for nare to nothing. Watch your backside."

After two more rest stops, San Francisco starts to make herself known. The air is filled with smoke from the houses and businesses. Homesteads, farms, stables and other man-made structures replace the forests. They top a ridge and there it is, San Francisco, buildings, haze, sailing ships, and people everywhere.

Ollie puts his full weight onto the friction brake to slow the wagon as they start down the hillside. "I suspect that wasn't the last gold coin you gave to Ojos."

"It wasn't."

"You'll be needin' a place to bed down and some clothes. The Frisco ain't fancy but it's clean and I know the owner. You can tell him I sent you. Those gold Yen won't be a problem either. Gold is gold. There's a dry goods store close by. It's far enough from the wharfs and bars to be somewhat peaceable. I'll swing by that way if you want."

"I appreciate the advice and the ride," responds Ocher. "The Frisco sounds just fine."

It takes a few kind words from Ollie to Honey Bee to get her assistance in making the side trip into town and the hotel. "How about some apples and carrots along with the oats tonight ladies? I need just a little cooperation."

People wave and greet Ollie as he navigates the team through town, finally arriving in front of a block-long building with a big painted sign stretching the length of the porch. *Frisco Hotel Clean Rooms.* Just as Ocher steps down and turns to say thanks for the ride, Ollie turns on the wagon seat to face the young man. "This here be Thursday. Come to dinner on Sunday noon. Ask anybody for directions." Without waiting for a reply, "Let's go, Honey Bee."

Chapter Ten

The Frisco is a two-story frame structure located north of the docks, warehouse, and business district. The traveler enters through a carpeted foyer. The fiber of the carpet feels soft and pliable under his bare feet.

The clerk looks up to see a young man needing a bath, haircut, shave, clothes and shoes. "Welcome to the Frisco. Will your luggage be along later? "

The man's tone is not condescending just inquisitive.

"I need a room. Ollie recommended you."

"Of course. Suite number seven, top of the stairs at the rear of the hall" the clerk hands Ocher the key. "That will be two dollars a night, in advance, please."

"All I have is gold Japanese Yen. Is that acceptable?

"Certainly, sir. For how long?"

"At least through Sunday."

The clerk makes the appropriate change and Ocher climbs the stairs.

Suite number seven is three rooms, a sitting room, a bedroom, and a small study. The rooms are clean and not accessible from the exterior of the hotel. Any visitor, friend or not, will have to walk the length of the hallway across the squeaky floor boards.

The traveler removes the cloth belt filled with jewels from his waist and hides it by removing the window sash, untying the counter weight and replacing it with the belt. He still has five of the Yen gold coins left, more than enough for clothes. Later he will convert the jewels to cash. He sits down on the edge of the bed. *I am an assassin not a thief. The jewels don't belong to me.* As he contemplates the implications of the jewels, his reverie is broken by a knock on the door.

"Who is it?"

"Message for you, sir."

Ocher opens the door to face a young boy holding out an envelope. Ocher takes the message and, before he can say thanks, the lad is gone.

Sir:
Your personal belongings and trade goods are in my possession. You may claim same at your convenience.
G. Stanley, owner
Stanley Shipping Co.

Ocher remembers Ollie saying that there are no secrets on the waterfront. Apparently news also travels quickly on the waterfront. Ocher looks down at his soiled and torn clothes and bare feet and decides it's time. He pulls a hair from the top of his head and places the hair in the door frame before closing it. If someone opens the door, the hair will be simply fall to the floor. He pads back down the stairs and out onto the porch looking for the dry goods store Ollie told him about.

Chapter Eleven

The shop owner of the dry goods store doesn't need to ask "How may I help you?" but he does. The answer is fairly obvious. Ocher has no shoes, torn and soiled clothes. In addition he needs a good scrubbing and a haircut.

There's a coordinated chaos as shirts, trousers, undergarments, shoes and hats are paraded past Ocher. He decides on two sets of clothing. Business attire and what he believes to be cowboy clothing including boots. He's never worn boots and never worn shoes until he left the jungle.

The shop owner suggests "The barber shop next door also has a hot bath available. I'm sure he would be glad to dispose of your current clothing."

Ocher nods.

"If you would choose one of the outfits I will have the other delivered to.... ?"

"The Frisco."

"The Frisco, certainly sir."

Ocher has accepted the fact that no one, at least so far, has turned down the Japanese coins. The shop owner accepts one without hesitation.

"Thank you, sir," he says handing Ocher the parcel of new clothes.

He walks to an adjacent barber, parcel in hand, to the shop advertising hot baths. "In there," is all the barber says when Ocher enters. "My man will bring in the hot water directly. Hope that's a new set of clothes," he says pointing his scissors at the bundle.

Up to this point the traveler has been bathing in cold mountain streams, scrubbing with river moss and shaking himself dry. The attendant bringing the hot water takes a long hard look at the tattoo on Ocher's chest but says nothing. The hot bath with real soap ain't bad. After toweling off he dons his new business clothes. The shoes are cumbersome. He decides that San Francisco society would think him foolish wearing a business suit and being barefooted. He accepts cumbersome.

The big grandfather clock in the dining room is chiming exactly seven when the traveler returns to the Frisco, just in time for supper. Ocher smiles thinking, *just as I was getting used to ships bells*. A quick scan of the room shows six men, each at a separate table and two women sitting together.

"Evening," he says as he passes the ladies headed to the last empty table. On the table there are forks, spoons and knives of different sizes and designs, none of which he has ever seen or used. He's learned many skills involved the art of killing, but not much in the art of fine dining. Time will tell.

The aroma coming from the kitchen area almost overwhelms the smell of the liquid the barber doused over Ocher and his new clothes. He knows the scents of the jungle, the forest, sweat and women's perfume. But this smell of the concoction poured on him at the barber is not appealing.

"Have you made a decision, sir?" asks a small, thin man who has materialized next to Ocher.

Before he can consider the question he answers, "About what?"

"Your meal sir. What would you like to eat?" the small thin man takes a half step backwards. "Been to the barber shop have we?"

Ocher smiles, "Yes. Don't care for the smell either. Next time I'll know. What would you suggest, sir?"

"The name is Sidney, not sir, Sir," Sidney says with a smile.

"Ocher, not sir, Sidney," returning the smile.

"The fried chicken is excellent, Sir Ocher. The chicken comes with mashed potatoes, gravy, fresh corn and biscuits of course. Would you like a whiskey, beer or wine with your meal?"

"I'll have the chicken but no alcohol. Do you have tea?"

"Hot tea or sun tea? Sun tea also goes well with the meal."

"I'll try the sun tea on your recommendation."

"Excellent choice, Ocher."

The meal is served promptly. The traveler's, first dilemma presents itself when the food arrives. Some of the men are using their hands to eat the chicken. One man is pointing what appears to be a leg at an adjacent diner apparently emphasizing some fact in their discussion. The women are using a knife and fork.

The clock chimes the quarter hour.

He decides that using one of the biscuits as an eating utensil would not be acceptable. Hunger wins out and he uses his hands for the chicken. He chooses the big spoon for the side dishes, taking great caution not to spill gravy onto his new clothes.

Sidney returns when Ocher has devoured everything within reach. "Pie? I recommend it."

"No thanks. I can hardly move after your last recommendation."

"Are you staying here at the hotel?"

"Yes."

"Just sign the bill and when you leave you can settle up."

Ocher hesitates and signs the bill the way he thinks Ocher should be spelled, "Is breakfast as good as this, Sidney?"

"Ever had flap jacks?"

"No."

"Then you're in for a treat. See you in the morning, Sir Ocher."

Ocher retires to his rooms. The hair is exactly where he had placed it. Before turning in, he levers a chair under the door knob and places a glass on the upper window sash, making trip alarms.

Chapter Twelve

"Good morning, Ocher, tea or coffee?"

There had been coffee on the *Anna Belle,* but he didn't trust the look of the black brew so he stuck with his tea during the voyage. Deciding that it's time to change and adapt to the local custom, "I'll have coffee and flapjacks."

Sidney delivers the coffee, "Cream and sugar are on the table." He whispers, "Use the small spoon."

Ocher's learns very quick that the coffee certainly has more bite than tea. He doesn't add anything to his tea so he adds nothing to his coffee eliminating the use of the small spoon.

The flapjacks are as recommended. Ocher has two helpings with a slice of ham each time.

His meal ends and with a full stomach Ocher steps out of the Frisco onto the walkway. The odor of his clothes has abated somewhat and the breeze is in his face so he takes a deep breath. He can smell the sea, aroma of cooking, wood smoke and the remnants of passing animals. He turns toward the smell of the sea. According to Sidney, Stanley Shipping is located in the wharf district among the warehouse and piers of San Francisco.

For each foray into this experience of America he studies the language and mannerisms of those he encounters. It's confusing, especially here. There's such a mix of sailors, business people, and cowboys. The speech patterns vary from very formal, *I will not do that*. Or changing words completely, *I won't do that*. Or just plain *nope*. He decides listening is far more important than speaking, for now.

Taking heed from Ollie's warning he watches for followers and the too casual observers while he strolls downhill. He has the feeling that he's being watched but can't locate anyone paying extra attention. The day is pleasant and he's in the open.

In the distance, he can hear the clamor of the offloading of ships, "Heave to on that vane line, make her fast to that bit..." Close by two men are arguing over the price of fish, "I won't pay over a dollar per hundred weight..." He remains vigilant but not worried.

The one-story brick structure appears to be well-maintained and relatively new. A sign affixed to the right of the door states simply *Stanley Shipping Lines*. Adjacent to the door on the left is a figurehead of a mermaid with flowing hair. Something about the carving catches Ocher's eye. It takes a moment before he realizes that on the left side of her fluke is a small engraving. Exactly like the tattoo on his shoulder. The answers to his questions are through the door and not outside.

Ocher enters through large double doors made from cargo hatches into a dimly lighted room with a solitary desk and several chairs. The entire outer office is furnished from ship works including the teak deck. The desk is located behind a ship's rail, where a man with heavy jowls and florid face is working over a ledger. He peers out from under his visor "May I help you?"

Ocher steps to the front of the desk, "Yes, would it possible to see Mr. Stanley on a personal matter?"

The man places his pen in an ink well, looks at Ocher and, without changing his expression, slides out of his chair. The man standing is no taller than when he was sitting. Without comment he turns and walks to the door directly behind him. He knocks then enters through the open door. He returns, swings open a gate in the ship's rail. Again without any change of facial expression, "Mr. Stanley will see you."

The little man's chair squeaks as he ascends to the peak of his chair and resumes work on the ledgers.

The inner office is elegant with dark wood paneling, teak decks covered in oriental rugs with the pleasant odors of cigars and leather. The man behind the expansive desk appears to fit the room exactly. Taking a puff on a cigar the elegantly dressed man takes the time to appraise Ocher. "I am Gregory Stanley. Won't you be seated?" pointing to a leather chair in front of the desk. "A personal matter?"

Ocher reaches into an inner pocket of his jacket and produces the note. "You are holding some of my personal effects as well as some of my trade goods."

Mr. Stanley doesn't respond immediately. "Yes, your belongings are safe."

"How did you come by them?"

"The *Anne Belle's* steward hid your personal belongings."

"The trade goods I purchased in Japan and loaded aboard the *Anne Belle*?"

"The goods are safe. And until I can determine your intentions here, they will remain in my possession."

Ocher sits back in the chair, "I have been told that you are a man of no nonsense. But this, sir, I would consider complete nonsense. You have no right to hold my property."

Gregory leans forward and tips the ash of his cigar into an ash tray. "Legally, you are correct Ocher, but morally I have an obligation to... again not your concern."

"How do you know...."

Gregory interrupts, "I know your name, I know about your tattoo and I know what you are. There are no secrets...."

Ocher interrupts, "On the waterfront, I have been told."

"I have nothing else to discuss with you at this time, Ocher. One question, is the Crow

Indian, Ojos I believe, with you? I owe him wages."

"No, he is traveling home to his family."

"Well, I will figure something out for him. For now, I will give you the benefit of some advice. Captain Quarte and the entire crew are no longer employed by my company. True or not, some of that lot will blame you for their status. Be aware."

Ocher stands and leaves in silence then stops just outside the shipping office doors to let his eyes adjust to the light and to assess his surroundings. All seems quiet except, there's someone watching him. He can feel it. *Where?* The street and the crowd seem normal. Someone's watching.

I thought I could escape. Already I'm being watched but by who? Is Mr. Stanley a friend or an enemy? The jewels. I will do as I was trained to do, observe.

Instead of going directly back to the Frisco, he meanders through the city stopping suddenly, changing directions, going into stores with multiple entrances, even stopping for coffee and pie. He doesn't look for specific people just patterns. When he stops who else stops, when he changes direction who else does the same? The watchers are good but inexperienced.

It's the street kids. Once he recognizes the pattern he also recognizes that the kids are too clean for their roles as street kids. *Whose kids?*

Chapter Thirteen

Saturday is spent leading his watchers around the streets of San Francisco. Ocher suspects he knows exactly who the watchers are, after a conversation with Sidney. He spends the day purchasing goods based upon that conversation. He is so focused on leading around the watchers he overlooks the sheer volume of his purchases. *I can't carry all of this out to Ollie's.* Before letting his watchers quit for the day he leads them to a livery stable and rents a carriage to transport their packages.

Sunday breakfast consists of his favorite meal, flapjacks. Ocher returns to his rooms, repackages the previous day's purchases, checks the trip wires and departs for Ollie's. The carriage is waiting for him. It takes several trips up and down the stairs to retrieve all of the packages. His expertise in carriage driving is minimal, but the horse is an expert. The horse maneuvers through the other street traffic dragging the carriage and Ocher along. With just minor coaxing the road to Ollie's is determined. The ride takes about half an hour.

The Oliver Von Derr's farm sits on fifty acres just at the foothills northeast of San Francisco. The house is a three-story, clapboard structure painted white sitting back from the other buildings. The barn, stables, and bunk house, although not painted, show a great deal of care. Twin stone pillars mark the path to the main house. A simple hand lettered sign is wired to the pillar on the right *Ollie's*.

Ollie stands peacefully with his head bent down under the eve of the porch watching his "kids" approach. "Welcome. I see you found the place."

"As you said, everybody knows where Ollie's is. The home for abandoned boys. I met some of them the last couple of days."

"Come, sit, have some cider."

One of the older boys who Ocher has seen over the last couple of days delivers a tray with cider. The boy lingers, wanting to hear what the grownups are saying but one look from Ollie and the boy leaves.

Ollie pours and hands Ocher a glass. "I'm not surprised you caught them watching you. After what I saw at the way station, I wasn't sure you needed protection. Captain Quarte is not to be taken lightly. The boys were just watching your back. How many did you see?"

Ocher takes a sip of the cider and sets down the glass. "I saw seven but I learned there are eleven boys. Pointing toward the buggy, there are some clothes, candy and presents for all of them."

"You are good. Seven was the numbers that were watching. The other four are too big and stand out. The clothes are appreciated. Eleven boys go through a lot of clothes, even with hand-me-downs. Marta will be pleased. Thank you."

"I understand you have two sons of your own along with the boys that are here?"

"Yes, they've just finished school in the East and will be home next week. One studied law and the other numbers. It'll be good to have them home. Some of the boys have never met them but are looking forward to seeing their big brothers."

A small blond head appears just outside the massive front door. "Papa O, dinner is ready."

Ollie stands and gathers up the packages. "Time to meet the family."

Chaos is the only term that can be applied to the scene in the dining room kitchen area of the house. Some of the boys are trying to set the table while others play tag, argue and fuss about. The scene is akin to a street brawl.

The woman in the kitchen calmly turns, picks up a wooden spoon and taps it lightly on the sideboard. The mayhem stops immediately. A well-practiced routine of setting the bowls, plates of food and pitchers of drink begins in quiet harmony. "Welcome to our home, I am Marta. You will sit there." She points to a chair next to the head of the table.

Ollie just smiles. "Don't let those blue eyes and blond hair fool ya. Marta can strike as quick as a rattler with that spoon, just ask the boys."

Ocher doesn't grasp the scale of Mr. and Mrs. Van Derr, until she stands next to Ollie at the head of the table. If Ollie is seven feet tall Marta is only slightly less. His massive hulk is in sharp contrast to her slim statuesque body. Her blue eyes sparkle with mischief and from the looks of the boys around the table, she is adored by them all.

All of the boys, except one, stand next to their assigned places. A blond, freckled-faced youngster stands and holds the chair for Marta. After she is seated, everyone else takes a seat. Conversation seems to float around the table. Not the scene one might expect with a gathering of this size. Ocher is at the center of the curiosity.

"Where you from? What do you do? Where are you going? What's your last name?"

Ocher answers the inquires as honestly as he can. "I am from an island in the Philippines. I am in the import business. I want to go to a place called Texas. First I have to go to Salt Lake City in the spring. Just call me Ocher."

The bowls of pichelsteiner, one pot stew according to Marta, are consumed. The dishes are gathered by the boys and transported to the kitchen. There a team of dishwashers scour the dinnerware and hand the plates and bowls off to boys with drying towels, then pass the dishes to the transport team for storage in a big china hutch. The silverware goes through the same treatment.

Ollie picks up two mugs and a coffee pot, "Join me in the parlor, Ocher."

Two older boys, introduced as Brady and Todd, join Ollie and Ocher in the parlor. The smaller boys can be heard out in the side yard divvying up the knives and candy.

Brady, a stocky boy with the arms and shoulders of someone used to hard work, "Papa O, is Ocher going with us to Salt Lake?"

Ollie smiles, "I don't know, Brady. Let's ask him. Ocher, I have a contract to deliver several wagon loads of goods to Salt Lake in the spring. Would you like to go with us?"

Ocher starts to respond.

"Before you answer, you have to know that between now and when we leave we have to build the wagons. You'll be expected to help and you won't get paid until when and if we make delivery."

"Let me understand this. I can accompany you on your journey if I build my own wagon while putting up with this tribe of rascals?" Ocher says with a smile.

Ollie looks over his coffee cup at Ocher, "All I can offer is room and board. There's a tack room in the barn with a bunk and you'd have to endure Marta cooking. You'd have to deal with the boys, however, on your own terms."

"Endure my cooking?" Marta says entering the parlor holding a tea service. "You don't have to be endure my cooking, Oliver Van Derr."

"I was just...."

"I know what you were just..." She sits next to Ollie on a couch built for four but Ollie fills most of it. Setting the tea service on a side table, she pours a cup then adds cream and sugar.

"Ocher, you'd be welcome here anytime with or without building a wagon."

Ollie starts to speak but quickly stops after a blazing glare from Marta.

"Thank you, Mrs. Van Derr."

"Marta."

"Thank you, Marta. I do have some town business to attend to but if the offer is still open after my business is completed, the tack room it will be. I can handle the boys just fine, I think."

Chapter Fourteen

"Good morning, Sidney, any recommendations for breakfast?'

"I believe I can come up with something. Coffee?"

Ocher nods.

"Mr. Stanley would like to meet with you at your earliest convenience," Sidney says as he pours the coffee.

Ocher nods again. "Ok."

Ocher is lost in thought throughout the meal. The same questions that have been filling his head since he arrived in America. *My goods, I would like to sell them. The jewels, what do I do with them? What is it I really want? Who can I trust?*

"Thank you, Sidney. Your recommendation is as good as ever," although Ocher can't remember what he has eaten, something about gravy and biscuits.

"The same small man, in the same chair with the same expression meets Ocher as he enters Stanley Shipping. Ocher poses the same question. "I would like to see Mr. Stanley, on a personal matter."

"Ocher, please join me," comes from the inner office.

Mr. Stanley offers Ocher a cigar which he declines. "I have a dilemma. I also have a solution. That solution you won't like. I can't let your likes or dislikes influence what must be done."

"Mr. Stanley, since I have arrived you have been less than cordial. In fact you have been down right meddlesome. You have held hostage my trade goods and expect me to show up at your summons. I don't care for it much. I demand that you release my goods or buy them. Then stay out of my business."

"Fine, I will buy them on one condition. You must leave and I mean today."

"No, Mr. Stanley, I intend to stay. In the spring Ollie has offered me the opportunity to accompany him and his sons on a trip. That is what I intend to do."

"I know all of that. Ollie is the problem."

For the first time in a very long time Ocher is on the verge of losing his temper. In his mind, he has already reached across the desk and taken Mr. Stanley by the collar and dragged him over the desk. Ocher takes a deep breath and relaxes his clenched fists, "Ollie is becoming more than an acquaintance. He couldn't possibly be a problem. You'll have to explain that."

"Ollie is a business partner of mine. More importantly, he is a friend. I consider them all as my family. By staying out at Ollie's you are putting them in the cross hairs of Captain

Quarte's and Gunter's revenge against you. I won't have it. You must leave."

Ocher sits back and takes another deep breath. "Mr. Stanley, we finally agree on something. I would never do anything to bring harm to Ollie, Marta and the boys. I will leave, today."

Gregory Stanley takes a long hard look at Ocher and starts to speak but stops.

"Is there something else on your mind, Mr. Stanley?"

"During your first visit here I told you I knew what you were."

"Yes, I remember."

"I didn't really know for sure until someone saw your tattoo. Then I knew for certain."

"The bath house."

"Yes. I have been bothered by your presence here but, more importantly, why are you here?"

"Why are you concerned?"

"My father."

"Your father?" Ocher pauses considering the implications. "The figurehead, the engraving, your father?"

"Yes. He escaped, came to America to hide."

"Your mother, this company and your father?"

"You get right to it don't you, Ocher? My father stole from the Tong. Well, he stole from a subject of a contract. He was supposed to return to the Tong with the stolen property. He didn't. He met my mother while working on a ranch in Arizona. The Indians burned the ranch. Mom and dad escaped and fled to the mountains where I was born. She died of consumption when I was eighteen. Dad sent me here with a deposit slip. I started this business on stolen money."

"Where is your father now?"

"Out there somewhere, hiding. I hear from him now and again. Is that why you're here Ocher, to hide?"

Ocher considers the question and decides to trust Gregory, "Yes, and I wish somehow to destroy them."

"You sound a lot like my father. That is or was his goal. Time has slipped away. He is just one man. Skilled yes, but aged. He would probably agree that it's your mission now."

"I need time to consider my future. I have to be alive to do that."

"I understand, Ocher. Go and let things cool down here. Gunter and Quarte have many enemies. Their futures will be determined by their own pasts."

"Will you explain things to Ollie? I mean about leaving, not the rest of it?"

"I will."

"Thank you."

"Your goods are worth one thousand dollars. There's an afternoon stage headed south. Come back at two o'clock and I will have gold and silver coins for you. Coins are easier to spend than script. One last thing. You can't go by just one name, it is suspicious. You'll need a surname. A common name would be best."

"What would you suggest?"

"How about Jones. Ocher Jones sounds good, don't you think?"

The assassin hesitates. Only a short time ago he was haunted by being the Little Orphan. Now with the help of two friends he has a name, a name of his choosing. "Ocher Jones it will be."

Chapter Fifteen

Ocher steps out of the building, stops to let his eyes adjust, appraises the surroundings and turns toward the Frisco. His feelings are in turmoil. He doesn't want to leave because of Ollie and family. But, he doesn't want to stay because of Ollie and family. The key here is family. Ocher knows the meaning of family but has never experienced a family. What he does know is being an assassin. *I wish to leave that life behind. I want to experience a family. I will leave, but I will eliminate those who stand in my way.*

Having made the decision he also makes a plan. Lure Captain Quarte and Gunter away from San Francisco, eliminate them and return. Leave a clear path for them to follow. On more than one occasion and from multiple people, he's been told there are no secrets on the water front. So he will make no secret of his intentions and his destination. *You want revenge, come and take it.*

Ocher enters the emporium where he has purchased his clothes and the clothes and gifts for Ollie's boys. "I will be heading south this afternoon and I require a satchel." Just outside the store, loafing in the shade, are several men of the sea. They are burned by the sun and wind, unshaven, leering at all who pass and sharing a bottle of some kind. Ocher's request is loud and aimed at the door. As he leaves with his purchase, he turns to the men, "Give my regards to Gunter. I'm pulling out."

Before returning to his room to pack, he enters the dining room. "Sidney, I need a favor."

"If it's legal, certainly, Ocher."

"Can you, somehow, get the word spread around to Quarte's and Gunter's friends that I got scared and have decided to run? I will be leaving on the afternoon stage headed south."

Sidney looks at Ocher apparently contemplating what to say. Finally, "That's a shame, the chef is preparing shepherd's pie for supper."

"What kind of dessert is that?"

"It's not a dessert, Ocher. It's a meat dish with potatoes."

"Sounds inviting, mighty inviting but I'm getting out of town. Gunter has scared me off."

"I'll see that the word is passed around, but..... You run scared? Not likely from what I've heard. But I'll do as you ask. You know they won't let it go." Sidney turns to leave, stops and turns. Smiles at Ocher, he says "Devious sir, but remember so are they."

It doesn't take long to pack. It takes longer to retrieve the jewels from the window sash. Before securing the jewel laden cloth belt under his shirt, he removes one green jewel and places it in his pocket. He settles his bill and leaves an envelope for Sidney, a gift of a ten dollar gold coin.

At the Wells Fargo stage office, "The afternoon stage, where is it headed?"

"Los Angeles is the last stop. The stage makes several stops to exchange horses and give passengers a break. But Los Angles is the only stop of any size."

"One ticket to Los Angles it is. How long a trip is it?"

"Two days more or less. The stage leaves at three o'clock."

Ocher takes his satchel and walks back to Stanley Shipping. The little man usually in the outer office is missing. "Is that you, Mr. Jones?"

Ocher doesn't reply. He enters the office feeling comfortable enough to sit down without being invited. "I still don't like having to leave. I agree that its best, but I don't like it."

"Let's not take any chances with Ollie's family. Take the stage. Quarte and Gunter, well as I have said before, their reputations and actions will lead to... well let's leave that unsaid."

Ocher hears bells from the ship's clock in the outer office indicating it is two-thirty, "One last thing, Mr. Stanley." Ocher reaches into his pocket and produces the green stone. "Whatever they need, make sure they get it. If you sell that and don't use the money for Ollie I will find out and you will pay."

Gregory Stanley pushes the green stone around his desk blotter with his index finger. "I didn't anticipate this," he says picking up the stone and sitting it back down. "Ocher, I think you have more problems than Quarte and Gunter. If you have more of these, and I suspect you do, our friends at the Tong will want them. There will be bounty out for you, unless. The fire in Japan..."

"I must be going," Ocher stands ending the conversation, nods toward the stone, "For Ollie."

Ocher steps from the dark interior of Stanley Shipping and as always hesitates to let his eyes adjust. Thinking, *Where I would be?* He looks across the street as he steps off of the walkway stumbling to the left. His initial thought is, *sooner than I thought.*

This is the second time a bullet has come his way. The first time he experienced the sound resulted in a long swim. The bullet strikes the ship's figurehead right where a bellybutton should be. Ocher's attention is drawn to a warehouse across the street. There's movement in a second story window. A second shot resounds, not quite as loud. This report comes from within the warehouse. A silhouette fills the window. A third shot rings out from Ocher's left, the sound coming from around the side of the shipping company building. The bullet finds its target and the figure in the window shudders from the impact.

"You need to step back inside," Gregory Stanley says.

Ocher, without taking his attention from the warehouse window, shakes his head.

A fourth shot rings out, again from the interior of the warehouse. The silhouette topples through the window. The man with a rifle in his hand crashes onto the small walkway awning and plunges onto the street, a big man.

The front door of the warehouse opens and a man dressed in a business suit wearing a bowler hat emerges holstering a revolver under his suit jacket. There's a badge affixed to the left lapel of the jacket.

The little man, the bookkeeper, appears from around the corner of the building carrying a large rifle, the weapon as tall as he is. Casually strolls past Ocher, "Mr. Jones."

Next to Ocher, Gregory Stanley addresses the little man, "Thank you, Maurice. Nice job."

"Thank you, sir."

The man from the warehouse walks straight to Ocher, "Mr. Jones, I am the Chief of Police. Glad to make your acquaintance."

Gregory Stanley walks past Ocher and extends his hand to the chief, "Thanks, Kevin."

"Certainly, Greg. We don't need riff raff like Gunter there shooting the good citizens of San Francisco. Thanks for the tip. Ah, here comes the clean-up crew now," The sound of a bell clangs in the distance.

Kevin offers a nod, turns to meet the arriving police detail. Ocher peers into the office at Maurice then returns his gaze to Greg. "Bait?"

Chapter Sixteen

"That's correct, Ocher. Bait. The question is who baited the hook?" Gregory says from behind his desk after relighting his cigar. "You certainly made every effort at presenting yourself as bait. We just took advantage of your work."

"But that only flushed out Gunter. What about Captain Quarte?"

Gregory smiles, "The good captain had a bit too much to drink last night. When he awakes he will find himself somewhere between here and Sitka, Alaska on a fishing vessel."

"You Shanghaied him?"

"No, absolutely not. He will be in command. At least until Sitka, where he will probably abandon his post and find passage back here. Should take several months. At least until you leave for Salt Lake City in the spring."

"Now what, Mr. Stanley?"

"On a personal level I'm sure the Van Derr's will welcome you. Ollie will be more than happy to teach you how to build a wagon and then teamster it north."

"I will welcome that as well."

"The jewel, do you want it back?"

"No."

"Ocher, there is a lot of money in California right now because of the gold fields. People are looking for investments. Like jewels. If you have more of them you may consider converting some of them to currency. Money is a lot easier to utilize than a precious stone. Give it some thought."

"I'll give it some thought. Now I need to go get my room back 'til Sunday."

"Already done, Sidney took care of that."

"Is this what it feels like to have friends, Mr. Stanley?"

"That's up to you, Mr. Jones. By the way, lucky you stumbled out there."

"Mr. Stanley, are you sure I stumbled?"

"Friends call me Greg, Mr. Jones. You don't strike me as the stumbling type."

"It's Ocher to my friends, Greg."

Chapter Seventeen

"Ocher, that's a mighty good looking wagon. She's straight, plumb and the wheels seem to be round," Ollie pronounces after his walk around inspection. "She might make it to Salt Lake. It's the teamster that might not make it."

"I still got a week to practice with the mules. Besides I got Gordon beside me. He'll keep me on the straight and narrow." Ocher responds, removing his protective apron and hanging it up.

"All kidding aside, Ocher, you done yourself proud with that wagon. You did a decent job on the carpentry and fashioned the leather work real well. You could even make a decent wainwright in a couple of years." Ollie laughs as he points to Ocher's on the belly. "You seem to have taken to Martha's cooking as well."

"Too good with the cooking. Had to buy new clothes, must have put on ten pounds. I suspect some of that was from swinging that hammer at the anvil."

"Speaking of cooking, let's follow the boys up to the house. Supper's ready. We're done out here." Ollie follows Ocher's example and hangs up his leather apron.

"I'm going to miss sitting at your table, Marta." Ocher realizes his mistake too late. Marta eyes begin to mist. She dabs at the tears with the dish cloth she is carrying.

"Go on sit down. Ocher, I made your favorite, *Jaegerschnitzel*, pork cutlets with fresh mushrooms. Enjoy, soon you'll be doing your own cooking. If you think enduring my cooking is a chore, wait 'til you have to eat Ollie's."

"Marta, I'll miss you more than the cooking, I'll miss you most of all and may even miss some of the boys."

A whoop of protests sounds from the assembled boys almost in unity but just as quickly stops when Marta reaches for her wooden spoon.

Ollie remains silent. Ocher has learned to read Ollie's silences and knows the big man will miss Marta a great deal on the two months long journey. "I won't be going on these long trips any more. This will be the last one. The boys are old enough to take over, if that's what they want."

The talk around the table is subdued in contrast to the usual lively back and forth. The normal brotherly taunting about the pending adventure has given way to reality. The brothers will soon be separated.

"Tomorrow being Sunday, our last Sunday together for a while, we will take a day of rest. Monday we will take all of the wagons to town and load supplies and the goods going north. It will take at least two days to repack everything, so we will leave on Thursday morning, early."

"Papa O, you sure I can't go?" asks the youngest boy, Vernon. "I won't take up much room. I won't eat much either. I promise."

"Vernon, you have a much more important job. You have to stay here and protect the farm, the other boys and your mother. I'd say that is a pretty important job, don't you agree?"

"I guess so, but I sure do want to go."

"There will be other trips and other adventures, but for now I need you here." Ollie reaches over and tousles the boy's hair.

After supper Ocher retreats to the tack room and his quarters. He has packed, unpacked and repacked all of his gear more times than need be. He wants to go and he wants to come back. Not like the *family* in the jungle. When he left there he never wanted to go back.

"Uncle Ocher?"

"Yes, Vernon."

"I really want to go. Would you please talk to Papa O for me?"

"Vernon, I know you want to go and you would be great help on the trail. But if you go who is going to take care of farm? You may be the youngest but all the other younger boys look up to you. Marta depends on you and Papa O trusts you to take care of things. That's pretty important wouldn't you say?"

"Yes, sir, I guess so, but..."

"I understand, Vernon, but it's important that you stay."

"Yes sir. Uncle Ocher, I'm gonna miss you."

Before Ocher can respond Vernon runs from the tack room. There, right there, that's what I want. To be missed by someone. Missed by a family, a family of my own.

Chapter Eighteen

Monday morning is a festival of absolute confusion fueled by coffee and doughnuts. The mules are lead out and hitched into the traces, wagons aligned in the order of the trip. "Where's this, where's that, did you see my..."

Ollie steps in, "All right enough. In one minute you will stand by your wagon. One minute or ..." The assembled "teamsters" know there is no "or", but are grateful for order being restored.

Finally the caravan starts toward town, first to the warehouse where the freight for Salt Lake is being stored. Next stop, necessities: groceries, cooking supplies, blankets, medicines, just in case, gloves, ammunition, etc. Each member of the caravan is given twenty-five cents to spend on sundries, most of the boys settling on hard candy.

Ocher leaves his wagon under the watchful eye of Gordon, his co-driver and walks to Stanley Shipping to meet with Greg and settle up the wages owed to Ojos.

After going through the usual cordialities with Maurice, Ocher is admitted to the inner office.

"Morning, Ocher."

"Greg."

"Time is getting short. You ready?"

"Yes and no. I never had, well, any of this. Family, friends, people you can trust and rely on. In the jungle we were always pitted against one another. To the victor kind of thing."

"You've adjusted to civilization. Dad couldn't get the hang of it. After mom died he wanted no further part in it."

"Greg, I want to use the jewels to somehow destroy the Tong."

"You have made that abundantly clear, Ocher. But you have to make a decision. Build a new life here or go back to the old life. The only way to destroy the Tong is to go backwards. I don't think that's what you want. Is it?"

"No, but the jewels are nothing more than ballast stones."

"As I have said, convert part of them to other resources and put the remainder in a safe place to be used when and if they are needed. That's what my father did."

"I know, I know, your father and I are rich men based on what we have stolen. That makes us nothing more than rich thieves. I don't want the money or the jewels."

"Take time before making a wrong decision. Consider the good you could do with...."

"I know, believe me I know. You and I have covered this ground over and over. There are eight jewels left, sell four and find a safe place for the other four. Sell the emerald for Ollie and use it as needed for the family."

"You still haven't told Ollie any of this, have you?"

"No. I don't believe he would condemn me for anything but he might. I don't want to take that chance. He knows what I am now and that's the important thing, at least for the time being."

"Before you go, here are the wages Ojos is owed. And I think he would appreciate the rifle he was promised," Greg hands Ocher a brand new Sharpe's .50 cal rifle.

"I'll make sure he gets this. Thanks this is very kind."

"All right, Ocher, bring me the jewels tomorrow here at eleven and I will make the arrangements."

The following day promptly at eleven a man, slightly taller than Ocher's six feet, wearing a tailored suit, adorned with a tie and tie pin joins Ocher and Greg Stanley in the inner office.

"Ocher, may I present James K. Lugler."

"Mr. Lugler, I have other commitments. Let's get right to it." Ocher takes a small pouch from a side pocket and removes four stones and presents them to the well-dressed gentleman. The man moves toward the window and examines the stones in his hand with a loupe.

"Oh my!" He glances at Ocher, the loupe still in place then back to the jewels. "I didn't expect this quality, but that won't be a problem."

"Mr. Lugler, do not waste my time expecting me to negotiate with you over price. I know what the jewels are worth. I will not haggle."

The transaction takes one hour. Ocher will soon have money, something that he really has no interest in. The cash will be available at the First National Gold Bank of San Francisco. The jewels are to be transferred at the bank after the cash has been deposited. In addition, a safety box is arranged for the remaining jewels.

Ocher tries to put the burden of thinking about the jewels out of his mind, but knows better.

Chapter Nineteen

Ocher stands on the front porch as Marta stands in the yard holding him in a good bye embrace. She is a head taller and the tears on her face are falling on the top of his head. "You come back anytime," she says finally releasing him. "You take care of all of my boys on this trip." Ocher smiles up at Marta, then walks to the last wagon in the train, puts on his wide brim cowboy hat and steps up into the seat.

There are six wagons in the train. All but Ollie's lead wagon is brand new built, over the winter by Ollie, the boys and Ocher. Each weekday had been the same. Rise before dawn, work on the wagons until exhausted, eat and collapse in the tack room. As a result Ocher has gained ten pounds of hard muscle and grown an inch to an even six foot. Still a foot shorter than Ollie's two sons Jorge, the lawyer, and Jeremy, the accountant.

The trip to Salt Lake City to deliver dry goods is also a good excuse to hand-deliver Ocher to Ojos. The route is well planned and with the backing of Mr. Stanley, Ollie's Freight Line is making its first cross country delivery. Each wagon is commanded by one of Ollie's boys, Ocher now considered as one of the boys. The younger boys, thirteen and under, are left at home. The final debate about who would stay and who would go ends only after the intervention of Marta's wooden spoon.

Ocher, each of the boys, and finally Ollie give Honey Bee a nose scratch or rub before taking their position in the wagon train. The sun is just coming up as Ollie gathers his reins and gives the command, "Ok, Honey Bee, lead the way."

Marta and the younger boys stand by the gate and wave as the caravan passes. Ollie is first. Marta's tears begin to cascade. Next is Jeremy, then Todd, the oldest orphan, with Phillip as his side. Theo, the next oldest, accompanied by Martin is next. By the time Ocher, last in line, passes, Marta has run out of tears. She waves as Gordon tries not to cry.

The caravan stretches down the road with nine drivers total with thirty-six mules in harness and one extra animal with each wagon. Although Ocher trained by making local deliveries with the team, Ollie decides, "You'll be last in line, Ocher. Don't want you holding up the procession."

The route will take them south of Carson City to Walter Lake, then on to the Rock River. Following the river north to Emigrant Pass then through the Ruby Mountains will bring them to the salt flats with Salt Lake City on the far side. The procession is armed but mainly for hunting. "If someone wants this stuff that bad, we'll give it to them. Can't say it's worth killing or getting killed over," Ollie remarks when packing the guns.

The nine hundred mile journey will take forty days so they provision for sixty days and twelve men in case of an emergency, Ollie counting as four. Marta's spoon is overruled about the menu being packed. "We can take only what won't spoil. Besides most of the trip it's gonna be too hot to eat. The bare basics," Ollie decides, "Beans, bacon, jerky, salt pork, coffee and a little flour and sugar. The more we take in vittles the less room for water and feed for the mules."

The boys remain animated all Thursday, Friday and Saturday, treating the first three days as a camp out and picnic. The trail has remained level with plenty of water. The scenery is green with the blooms of spring all around.

It didn't take long to learn the temperament of some of the mules. No major damage, just a couple of the younger boys have been stepped on and Dustin is still showing teeth marks from the mule now called Shark.

On Sunday morning the reality of life on the trail makes its first appearance. During the planning stages of the trip, it's agreed by all that Sunday would be a non-travel day. "A day of rest," Ollie says.

Ollie neglected to say it would be a day of rest for the mules. Each mule is groomed, hoofs checked and pampered with a treat.

Around Lake Walter the prickly pear is in bloom so the boys are tasked with gathering the blooms. Ollie takes time to point out, "Don't reach and grab the flower, you'll get stuck with needles. Grab the flower at the top and use your knife on the bottom."

"Boys will be boys. Now you know why it's called a prickly pear, Gordon," Ocher shares while removing the spine.

The fresh sweet flowers are fed to the mules.

While the boys are out picking flowers and getting stuck with cactus needles, the men inspect all of the harnesses, traces, lead lines, yokes and wheels, continuing the day of rest. Before bathing is allowed the water barrels are filled. An inventory of food takes place.

Jorge promises, "You get your homework right the first time and you'll get a piece of rock candy." No one missed out.

"Bathe yourself and your clothes, with soap. It won't take long for your clothes to dry," Ollie directs. "Then rest a bit before supper."

Apparently fishing is resting, so everybody heads to the lake to catch supper. Most of the younger boys bathe again by shoving and pulling each other into the water.

During supper Ollie observes Jeremy, his oldest son, eating peaches from a quart jar. "I don't remember those being packed."

Jeremy smiles up from his sitting position, "Mom snuck them into everybody's pack. Said she didn't want us getting scurvy."

"We agreed only the basics, son."

"You agreed, and if you think I'm gonna disagree with my mother and that spoon, you can discuss that with her when we return."

Ollie shakes his head, but goes directly to his pack to see what Marta has snuck in.

Returning to the fire, "Don't throw away the jars. Fill them with water for the mules."

Monday morning the pure joy and jubilation of the start of the trip is gone. The grind of hitching, riding, caring for the mules and the absence of mom's cooking is setting in. Gordon doesn't bounce onto the wagon seat: he climbs in and settles down on the wooden seat. "I guess I'm ready."

Gordon and Ocher each take a hand at driving the team. The sixteen year old actually has more time driving a team than Ocher. "Is it like this where you're from, Uncle Ocher?' asks Gordon.

"No, not at all. It's hot like this but not as dry. The trees are very tall and the bushes are so thick you have to cut through them just to walk. And there are snakes, spiders and ants everywhere. It rains all the time and it's muddy."

"We have all of those crawly things here. I think I like this better. It seems fresh and beautiful in the spring. I know it won't be like this when we head back but right now it's real nice. How do you walk in boots if it's muddy all the time?"

"I never wore shoes until I got here, just bare feet. The boots are taking a while to get used to."

"Your friend, Ojos, is an Indian right?"

"Yes."

"He can teach you to make moccasins I bet."

"I bet he can. I'll let you know."

"Promise, Uncle Ocher?"

"I promise."

Gordon, sitting to Ocher's right, has just finished a slow turn to the left around a sand mound and is handing the reins to Ocher. "Uncle Ocher, look at the deer coming out of the Pinions over there." Ocher gathers in the reins. "Don't point. Just sit back." The red headed youngster has learned that Ocher's word is to be accepted not challenged, so he sits back knowing Ocher will explain.

"What do you think caused that, Gordon?"

Ocher pulls the lead slightly to the left so he can get a better view without turning in the wagon's seat. The deer don't stop and graze but just keeping moving parallel to the pinion grove. Then, without warning, they bolt over the hill out of the line of sight. Ever so casually Ocher brings the team back to the right.

"I believe there is someone out there."

Gordon whispers out the side of his mouth, "Yeah, I think so."

"I think we are being followed. Keep that under your hat at least for now. I'll see what Ollie thinks when we stop at noon." Gordon nods his head trying to remain as calm as Ocher.

Each day the caravan stops at around noon, typically where there is a small oasis with water still flowing from the snow thaw in the surrounding mountains. The mules are taken out of the traces so they can graze, get water, and roll around in the grass and sand. The men of the caravan tend to the needs of the mules and equipment first and then have coffee or water with a piece of dried beef.

After Ocher and Gordon take care of their mules, they check the wagon. Ocher inspects Gordon's splinter site, "Even a small infection can cause problems in a hurry." Ocher goes to find Ollie.

Ollie is standing with several of his boys around the coffee fire getting the results of the ritual noon inspections. "No problems. Had to replace a shackle. Shark is still trying to bite....."

"Ollie, come and take a look at one of the wheels on my wagon." The big man drains the remaining coffee from his cup, sets the cup down on one of the rocks used to make a fire pit and heads toward the last wagon in the train. Ocher tries to keep up but each step of Ollie's is six of Ocher's.

"I don't see anything wrong with the wheels," Ollie says as Ocher arrives.

"There isn't, but keep looking. We're being followed. I got the feeling this morning, now I'm sure. I don't know how many, but one thing is for sure, they have to be white men not Indians. They've made too many mistakes. They are probably after the cargo."

Ollie straightens up and looks at Ocher with a grin on his big face. "Did you know that the boys have been having a contest with you since you arrived? The object of the contest is to see if anybody can sneak up on you. Well, sir, nobody has managed to do it. The reason you are last in line is not because of your driving skills. It's because nobody can sneak up on you and you've done it again. You have a plan, don't you?"

"Without making a big fuss of it, shuffle around the driving teams so that it will appear from a distance that all of the teams are intact. I won't be going with you. Today is Wednesday. Plan on being at the sand bogs on Saturday and leaving Monday. I'll meet you there before you get underway.

Ollie returns to examining the wagon wheel. "You sure?"

Ocher nods. "Yeah, I can move faster alone. If I need help, I'll come and find you. I'll get a canteen, some jerky and get going. See you at the sand bogs."

By the time Ollie and Jorge finish making a big scene about changing the wheel that doesn't need changing, Ocher is over a mile away. He has already set up a camp so he can watch the followers when Ollie and crew resume their move. Ocher notes that the train with the appropriate drivers looks as it should. Upon close inspection, the third wagon in line seems to have a pile of clothing next to the driver but to the casual observer it would appear to be a sleeping form.

The afternoon wears on and Ocher catches a nap when, as Ojos has always pointed out, the noise gives the followers away. There are twelve of them, certainly not twelve trail wise cowboys, but eleven wharf rats with Captain Quarte in the lead. *Welcome back, captain. Did you enjoy Sitka? Thinking of killing two birds with one stone? Get the caravan's cargo and get even with me? Captain, you should have stayed in your element and not ventured into mine.*

Quarte gives orders to set up camp, "You there, get some wood and get a fire started." "Break out some rations, get them started," he says to no one in particular.

Even from a distance Ocher can hear the grumbling of the men. "We ain't aboard ship and that albatross of a bosun ain't here."

This is not what they're used to. Working the docks is hard work with its own set of dangers. Out here this gaggle of men is not prepared or experienced for the dangers and pitfalls of the wild. The camp is set up incorrectly. There's no water source, no escape routes, the horses are left unprotected, the fire is too big and the biggest mistake is the liquor.

Ocher turns to see a lizard watching him and the camp below.

"You see what I see?"

The lizard doesn't answer but stays in position.

"I don't see any extra water or rations down there. Not even a pack horse."

The lizard nods up and down.

"Appears to be plenty of whiskey though."

The lizard turns and scampers to the shady side of the rock.

"Could use a horse," Ocher says to no one.

Ocher sits back in his cold camp and plans out the night's activities.

By sunset, the liquor has done a job on the tired and thirsty men. The captain has posted no lookouts around the camp or the horses, a fact that Ocher is counting on. He moves slowly around the camp, coming from the downwind side of the horses, and, as he makes his final approach, he begins to talk in low and comforting tones to the animals. The smell of the mules is still on him and his clothing, so the herd remains calm. There's no nickering or ground pawing, just interest in the new comer. Ocher picks out four horses, puts on the bridles and leads them away from camp. He takes them just beyond his camp site and returns to the snoring men. Like fog drifting through the camp, he uncorks all of the liquor bottles he can find, upends them, picks up the meager food supplies and drifts out of the camp taking two more horses and one saddle with him. By dawn he has taken the horses miles away to a lush grass valley with a small stream that the caravan has crossed. He releases all but one and returns to his cold camp just in time to watch the camp awaken.

The good captain is beside himself, kicking the men into action, pointing and screaming at anyone within his reach. His foul temperament increases when he realizes he has lost half his horses and the majority of his rations. In addition to what Ocher has inflicted on him at least one of the early risers within the group has sized up the situation and has run off with an additional horse. The captain is now down to four horses, six men and no supplies.

What now Captain Quarte? Ocher sees two options. One: give up and limp back to San Francisco. Two: try to catch up to Ollie and somehow mount a raid on the caravan.

The captain makes the decision to continue after the caravan. "Six of you will ride double, the remainder will walk. We will stop at noon and switch off." After a heated discussion the six biggest men ride double and the captain leads, riding solo.

After much cursing and grumbling the remaining four men set out on foot following the captain. Ocher notes that it's going to be a long and uncomfortable walk. These men are wearing shoes, good only for city streets, not boots with a thicker sole. Ocher steps into the saddle, and starts out cross country riding parallel to the captain.

The horses don't make it until noon. Carrying two men in the dry heat has exhausted all but Quarte's horse. The captain is relentless pushing the horses until finally one goes down. To complicate matters, one of the riders breaks an arm when the horse falls. The captain steps down and walks over to the downed horse and kicks the animal while tugging on the bridle to get the horse to stand. "Get up, you lazy beast," he snarls. The exhausted animal has nothing left to give and takes the abuse. Without warning the captain shoots the horse. Ocher is close enough to hear the captain demand. "You - fix his arm then catch up," pointing to one of the men that had been riding. He turns to the remaining men. "We'll walk the horses until noon."

Ocher sits just inside a tangle of rocks and scrub brush watching as the captain leads his procession away. He waits long enough for Quarte to get out of range then starts down the hill toward the two men. The larger of the two men has his back to Ocher and is tending to the smaller man's broken arm. Ocher removes the knife he always carries between his shoulder blades, walks right up behind the larger man, places the razor sharp blade against his throat. "Throw your guns and knives over toward the horse or die." Without hesitation the order is followed. Ocher steps back. "It would appear that the good captain has abandoned you."

"You Jones?" the big man asks.

"Yep."

"If you're here, them in the train knows they're being followed."

"Yep."

"Looks to me if we stay on this course and follow the captain we'll be high and dry.

"Yep."

"We ain't the type to abandon ship, but we ain't aboard a ship. The captain appears to have already abandoned us. Best me and Claude there head back to port."

"Yep."

"Could you help me set his arm?"

"Yep."

"When I come across my shipmates the captain has set afoot, we'll head back to Frisco."

"All right, but if any of you continue to follow the wagon train, I'll make sure the desert kills you slowly."

"Understood. We'll be headed to our home port."

Ocher helps the big man set Claude's arm. "One last thing. Some of your supplies are cached in the rocks about a mile due west of last night's camp site. The horses are gone, so don't waste your time looking for them. I've given you more of a chance than you and the captain intended to give us. Remember, you follow us and you will die." Without waiting for a comment, Ocher turns and disappears into the rocks and scrub brush.

Chapter Twenty

Trailing the captain and his men is easy. Every animal within a mile is fleeing from the approaching group. Just by watching the birds, coyotes and deer scatter, Ocher can stay out of sight and spare his horse. He doesn't want to get ahead of the troupe because he can't guess where they might camp overnight. It would be fairly easy to determine where a trail-wise group would stop, but not this bunch. He spends the day riding and walking, meandering through the high desert watching the scurrying animals.

The captain stops about a half an hour too late. The only correct decision is that he stops where there's water. "Gather up some wood and get a fire started," he says, but there is no one standing close by to receive his order. The men have all rushed to the small pool of water.

Out of the darkness, "Shouldn't we look after the horses, captain?" asks one of the men.

As an afterthought he does have one of the seamen unsaddle and set the horses loose. The horses immediately go to the water and then wander a short distance away to roll in the dirt. Ocher can see that it's going to be a long night for the captain and his men. They build a fire big enough to signal ships off shore, even with the ocean being several hundred miles to the west. The amount of wood needed to maintain the fire will keep the group busy all night. Ocher finds a comfortable spot in a small brush arbor, waters his horse, rubs him down with some dry grass and pickets the animal in an area of ground greenery. He makes one final check of the other camp noting that the captain has not assigned a guard on the horses. Laughing at their complete stupidity he takes the saddle blanket and curls up for a nap.

The men in the camp below have finally given up on keeping their bonfire blazing. The four men are huddled together in a lump with the saddle blankets lying on top. They haven't even bothered to cut pinion boughs to lie on the ground.

The sound of horse shoes on stone wakes Ocher. He snakes down to the camp to investigate. No need to waste a trip. He decides to liberate four horses but there are only three. He quietly checks the camp and sees that the sound that woke him was the captain sneaking out of the camp. He returns to the picketed animals with the intention of taking the horses but just shakes his head, returning to his own camp.

As Ocher is sitting in a tangle of creosote bushes having some jerky for breakfast, a scream of pure agony erupts from the camp. Ocher suspects he knows what has happened. Walking in the soft soled shoes has taken a toll on the men below. To ease the pain in their feet they have removed their shoes for the night. A cowboy used to the trail would have shaken out his boots to make sure nothing has climbed in during the night. Someone in the camp has made a serious error. He has put on his shoe without shaking it out. Ocher sneaks to the top of the ridge and looks down into the camp.

One man walks hurriedly to where the captain should be, "Looks like the captain's gone." Another of the men rushes toward the horses, "The horse he's riding ain't here."

Ocher had determined the night before that he was going to leave these men to the elements but now knows he can't just ride away. He works his way down through the scrub brush and boulders and walks into the camp with the sun at his back.

"You there," Ocher says to a tall gaunt looking gent standing over the writhing man. "See that bush yonder?" Ocher points toward a prickly pear cactus. "Go gather some of the ears. Trim off the thorns before you cut them off the bush." The man spins around, startled by Ocher's command. "If you want my help, get going." The man turns, stops, looks back, lowers his shoulders in defeat and stalks out of camp.

The man in agony is a big heavy-set man with a red bulbous nose and a leg now swelling to twice the proportion of the rest of him. He's moaning and trying to reach down to his swelling leg but his girth is preventing the attempt. "Lay still or you'll make it worse." Ocher looks around to account for the remaining men. A young man with a scar down his cheek is standing just out of Ocher's reach with a gun in his shaking hand pointed straight as Ocher. "Either shoot or get a fire started. If you shoot, you'd better kill me 'cause if you don't you'll be dead before the echo fades. Your choice."

The young man can tell from staring into the cold blue eyes that this man means what he says. "I'll get firewood." He lowers the gun and as he passes by Ocher, drops it on the ground.

"We're missing one. Where is he?"

The young man points toward the creek. "Went to wash up."

"He can help you with the fire."

The tall man returns with half dozen prickly pear ears. Ocher reaches out, takes one and splits it to expose the interior mucus-bearing fruit. "Give me your neckerchief," he says to the man with the injured leg. He ties the prickly pear over the sight of the scorpion sting. "I'll be right back." He walks up the hill to his camp, picks up the coffee, a cup and pot and returns to the four men in the lower camp. "Get some coffee on to boil," he directs them as he hands over the makings to the men working over the fire.

The men are wary of Ocher, but at least this man seems to know what to do

"Who are you, mister?" one of the men asks.

"Jones, Ocher Jones."

"You be the gent Quarte is after?"

"Yep. Good thing he didn't catch me."

"Suspect so," the man says. "If you did the things he says you done. Coffee?"

With a cup of fresh coffee in his hand Ocher walks over to the injured man. "If you were going to die, you'd have done it by now. Put a fresh piece of that prickly pear on that leg about every four hours. In a day or two you should be able to travel."

"A day or two, out here?" The man with the injured leg tries to stand and falls back to the ground. "A day or so sounds ok."

Ocher turns to the three men sitting around the fire drinking his coffee. The men are dusty, sun burned and Ocher suspects hungry. "You boys are land locked and in a heap of trouble. You got any plan on getting out of this country?"

The young man who had the gun, "You ain't going leave us out here like this are you?"

"Well, mister," Ocher begins, "you and your friends here were gonna do worse than that to our wagon train. So I wouldn't go passing judgment on my intentions." Pointing toward the fat man on the ground, "He won't be able to walk for several days, but he can ride. If it was me, I'd head due west to Carson City. With some luck you should make it in five or six days. This time of year there will be water enough and you can trap small game. Going south the way you came will take a site longer and that's probably the way the captain rode out. I'm guessing that if you caught up to him that would be your bad luck." Ocher walks over to the fire, pours himself a cup, dumps the rest on the ground, picks up his poke of coffee and walks out of camp, coffee cup in hand.

Ocher breaks down his camp and saddles the horse. "Well, let's see if we can cover some ground." The horse knickers as if he understands and the pair move out to the north, following a small stream. In the late afternoon just short of time to look for a camp, Ocher pulls up. "I swear I smell coffee." The horse is looking up stream and his ears have pricked up in the same direction. "Slow and easy. This ain't part of that bunch back there." He steps down, ties the reins to a bush and moves slowly toward the now distinct smell of coffee.

Chapter Twenty-One

A slim man, wearing well-worn buck skins, is sitting with his back against a large boulder, feet crossed holding a coffee cup in his left hand. In his right hand is a buffalo gun. The barrel is resting on the upper toe of the crossed legs, the bore pointing straight at Ocher. The man's fine grey hair is trying to escape out from under his cowboy hat. A blackened enamel pot is resting just within reach on a small smokeless fire. Next to the coffee pot is another cup. "Come on in if you're friendly. You wouldn't happen to have a bit of honey in your outfit would you?"

Ocher walks into the camp and points to the coffee cup. "You expecting company? And no, I'm traveling kind of light, no honey."

The man lowers the rifle to the ground, never taking his blue grey eyes off Ocher. "Just you? There's coffee if you want it. Too bad about the honey. I'm kinda partial to a drop or two in my coffee. "

Ocher pours himself a half cup of the thick black brew, sits with his back against an adjacent rock while taking a quick look around the camp.

He concludes from the gear, mules and demeanor that the man is alone.

"You followin' that wagon train?" the old man asks as he points with his coffee cup.

Ocher sees no harm in telling the man. "No, I'm with the wagon train. We were being followed."

The man shifts slightly on the rock and changes the position of his crossed legs. "Interesting choice of words, 'we were being followed.' I'd bet there is a mighty interesting story in there somewhere."

Ocher has been taught to trust his instincts. His instincts tell him to trust this old man. Over coffee and some dried jerky Ocher offers his name, then lays out the story. The man listens intently, just a chuckle slipping out now and then.

"Ocher, you might as well spend the night. You'll catch up with Ollie quick enough on horseback. I'll get some beans and salt pork goin' for a proper supper. You know what else needs to be done."

"You got a name?"

"Abel Jones."

The name stops Ocher for just a second. Gregory Stanley said that Jones is a common name.

During the cooking, eating and talking Ocher learns that Abel has wintered down in the Navajo Nation in a place he calls the Colored Sands. He's headed north to Salt Lake for provisions and then into the mountains.

"Civilization and me ain't on speakable terms. We tolerate each other when the need arises"

Long after sunset they move away from the fire and bed down.

Ocher already has coffee boiling when Abel rolls out of his blanket into the grey dawn. "Abel, our wagon train is headed to Salt Lake. You're welcome to join us. They are waiting for me at the sand bogs."

"I ain't ready for company yet, 'preciate the kindness. Would offer a piece of advice, take it or leave it. Most folks head east from the bogs. If you go northeast two days you'll find a string of three small fresh water lakes. You'll be two days further north with full barrels, could make a difference."

Ocher walks his horse down to the small pool of water letting him have one last drink. He steps into the saddle and rides just short of the camp. "It's been a pleasure, Mr. Abel Jones. Thanks for the company, coffee and conversation. Maybe we'll share a fire again." He heads the horse northeast toward the wagon train.

Abel holds up his cup in a salute. "You can bet on it."

Chapter Twenty-Two

Ocher isn't concerned about being followed, except by Abel. Ocher's instincts tell him he couldn't catch Abel at it anyway. He decides to take a straight course toward the sand bogs. Nevertheless, he occasionally stops, walks the horse and checks his back trail. At noon he stops to rest, let the horse roll in the dirt, and have a meal of coffee and jerky. The noon camp is well above and off the trail. The surrounding vegetation is sparse, so anybody moving around below is easily spotted, but no one is following. He keeps to the high ground, staying below the ridge lines, never silhouetting himself on the ridge tops. At sunset he rides into camp at the sand bogs.

Ollie is the first to greet him. "Nice horse."

Before Ocher can respond to Ollie, the boys come at him in an avalanche. "Who is following us? Are they gone? Did you have to fight anyone? Whose horse?"

Ocher just smiles. "Later boys, need to tend to my horse."

The big man wants to know all of the details but can't get a word in. "Supper's on."

The mules don't seem to mind just one horse. There's some stamping and assorted noise but that only lasts a minute. After Honey Bee takes a sniff and doesn't take a chunk out of the horse's hide, the herd accepts the newcomer. Ocher walks toward the cooking fire, glad to be back with his friends.

The whole camp wants to hear the details of the Ocher's adventure, but to their dismay the only thing he will say, "I just took their horses and set them afoot. They won't be following us anymore." It isn't the Saturday night story telling the boys wanted.

Sunday is the same with just about everybody wanting details but getting nothing. With so much Sunday work to keep their minds occupied, the troupe finally concedes and sets about Sunday's business of maintaining the wagons, equipment, mules and one horse.

The sand bogs are formed from snow run-off gathering in bowls of soft sand with minimal drainage. Not quite quick sand but close enough. The water coming into the bogs is fresh and clean. On Sunday each water barrel is emptied, scrubbed and refilled to the brim with fresh water. Ollie finally let's all hands relax after he inspects each barrel. Sunday's day of rest doesn't include much rest.

Ocher does share with Ollie his meeting with Abel and the suggestion of a more northerly route. By sundown Ollie has decided that he will take the northern route. "Full barrels make sense when crossing the flats, just good sense."

Although water is always a concern in the desert, it hasn't been a problem, until now. The run off has been providing streams and creeks on a pretty consistent basis.

But the desert changes and changes quickly. The two day trip north is dry. The run-off has been absorbed by the sands. The small pockets of water have evaporated or consumed by the desert wild life.

"Boys, don't waste a drop. The real trip begins now," Ollie repeats at the nooning.

Ollie allows only a mouthful of water to the men and then only after taking care of the livestock. "Mules first..."

"We know Papa O. Riding is better than walking," Gordon finishes.

Ollie measures every drop during the noon breaks and at night. Only one big pot of coffee is made and served with a minimum of food. "You drink more if you eat more." Ollie constantly reminds all within earshot. For Ollie, having minimum portions emphasizes the severity of his concern.

After two full grueling days, the mules smell the water. Ollie doesn't need to change course, Honey Bee makes her own decision. As soon as the caravan reaches the first lake, in unison the boys yell, "Mules first."

Around the evening fire Ollie answers the boys' questions, "It's gonna get worse, isn't it, Papa O?"

"Yes. You got a bit of taste in what's to come when we cross the salt flats. Boys, now we're gonna earn our wages."

There are three lakes as Abel had said "about half a day apart, then due east." The wagons are stopped at noon beside the second lake and a proper night camp at the third lake. Every available container is filled to the brim before departing due east.

Honey Bee stops short at her first glimpse of the salt flats. The spring runoff that sometimes accumulates on the flats has been absorbed or evaporated. Absolutely nothing is growing.

"What's that, Uncle Ocher?" Gordon asks pointing off to the north.

Ocher pulls out his telescope, "Just a rock, Gordon. How it come to be out here I couldn't guess."

The fascination of wanting to see the salt flats soon evaporates, just like the water. The boys don't seem to envy Ollie being in the first wagon and getting to "see things first." Out here there's nothing to see and it doesn't change. Just follow the wagon ruts ahead and don't think about being thirsty.

"Look, Uncle Ocher, everything looks white. The dust looks like snow. Wish it was."

"Be a sight more comfortable if it was snow," Ocher responds even though he has only seen snow and never been in it.

The fine layer of "snow" is fine dust tainted with salt. Licking your lips makes you thirsty; not licking your lips makes them split open. There's no sweat. It evaporates too fast.

At the noon break Ollie and Ocher walk away from the wagons to eliminate any influence of the steel on Ollie's hand-held compass. After looking back at the wheel ruts left behind the caravan, he turns to Ocher, "Due east, straight and true."

The mules are given a half of a cup of water. But only after having their mouths cleaned out by using a wet handkerchief, a job that's shared by driver's and co-drivers. No need to go off the trail to relieve yourself. There's nothing to relieve. Nobody wants to eat or have coffee, too hot to make a camp fire. Besides, the wood that was brought along has to be saved for a night camp. There certainly isn't any wood in the flats. The half cup, a ration of water, is all that's craved.

The wagon train halts just after sun down. The mules are tended to. Ollie considers making a fire for coffee but stops.

Instead he gives out a full cup of water to each of his teamsters and three pieces of hard candy. "We'll let the moon rise and then move on. It'll be cooler if we travel at night."

The mules don't seem to mind. They want out of the flats as bad as everybody else.

Gordon is leaning over resting against Ocher's shoulder just as the grey dawn wakes him. Ocher is transfixed on following the wagon ruts in front of him.

"Uncle Ocher, look." A minute black line is present on the horizon. By full sunup the black line has grown into mountains.

At the noon stop Ollie has coffee made and requires each person to eat something. "There's still a long way to go, boys, and you have to keep your strength up." There's no enthusiasm for eating and not much for drinking hot coffee in the one hundred degree heat.

When sunset finally arrives, the men, mules and equipment are all done in. There's no interest in eating. Ollie insists, "Have to keep your strength up. You'll be not good to anybody if you get too weak to pull your share. At least have a cup of coffee and..."

"Any of that candy left, Dad?" Jorge asks. "Hot sweet coffee sounds pretty good to me."

"Yes, there is. On one condition. Everyone has to eat some jerky with coffee or water in the morning."

"Deal," comes from the camp.

Ocher considers that they might need a night watch, but after looking around the camp no living creature in camp is awake. Even the mules are snoring. At dawn Ollie makes sure that his deal is observed. All hands have a cup of coffee or water and a piece of jerky.

Sometimes in the jungle the older men would smoke opium. The result would take the men away in their minds. They would walk about without focus. Ocher knows there's no opium here but the entire camp is operating on routine. No focus. Day after day the routine stays the same. Honey Bee trudges due east and the rest of the caravan follows in her footsteps.

At night even the grumbling is gone. Take care of the mules and listen to Ollie insist on food and water. Even the food is not changing. It's too hot to make beans and bacon with pan bread. It's too hot and too much of a chore to cook or eat.

Even making any attempt at comfort is gone. The wagon teams complete the routine of chores and then walk to their wagons, crawl under and collapse. If they make to their wagon.

"Uncle Ocher, I'm cold," Gordon moans almost every night. He's too tired to remember to get his blanket from the wagon.

The chill eats right through the exhaustion.

The snow-capped mountains seem to be mocking the caravan. At night they seem a little closer but at dawn they don't.

Ollie seems to diminish in size almost by the hour. His portion of water and food is the same as each man in the wagon train. His bulk needs far more but he won't take any additional rations.

"How many days has it been, Gordon? I can't keep track," Ocher asks.

"I'm sorry, Uncle Ocher. I can't remember."

After five or maybe six days the mountains begin to grow with each turn of the wagons wheels. Finally the ever-present sand dust is broken here and there with sage brush, rocks and real dirt. The mules can smell water. Honey Bee steps up her cadence but is too exhausted to maintain the pace. In the distance there are seagulls flying.

There is great jubilation in the train when Utah Lake comes into view. There are visions of camping next to fresh water, all you can drink and a proper supper. That dream is momentarily dashed when the legions of mosquitoes attack every warm blooded thing in the train. Camp is made several miles north of the lake along the creek feeding the lake. There's no water left in the barrels. The extra water taken on at "Able's Lakes" has made the difference.

Before Ollie can get the camp organized, the mules are unhitched. The mules and the boys including Ollie are knee deep in the stream stripping the salt-caked clothing off. The shirts are so coated that it's like trying to submerge a piece of wood. After a few minutes of soaking, the dirt turns to mud and then can be rinsed off. Without leaving the stream the shirts and pants are thrown into a big pile alongside the creek leaching out a white stream of salt dust. Ollie finally steps out of the creek, "Now boys, let's get some fire wood and get the camp set up. But first get your extra duds and dress. There's got to be civilization close by."

The mules apparently decide they will camp on the opposite side of the creek, and, after a few half-hearted efforts to get them to cross back to the human camp, the effort is abandoned.

There's coffee, beans with huge slices of bacon, pan bread coated with sugar and cinnamon. After too many days of coffee and exhaustion, water is the drink of choice. Jeremy gathers up all of the quart jars and makes sun tea. He's been saving the tea for such an occasion. There's a subdued celebration around the camp that night. Exhaustion hasn't overtaken the enthusiasm.

The entire crew is gathered around the fires drying out long johns, shirts and pants. The boys are taking great care not to soil their going-to-

town clothes. Civilization must be close by so guards are posted. It's an early evening.

Ocher and Ollie are standing just outside of the ring of wagons looking back toward the salt flats. "Rough eight days," Ollie remarks.

Ocher looks up at the big man. "I thought it was nine."

"Nope, just eight. I knotted a string each morning so I'd know. I'm mighty proud of all my boys. We didn't lose nobody. I was a bit troubled when you stayed behind. Now we know, now they know, they can do a man's job. Enough of this kinda talk. Best get some rest. Busy day tomorrow."

Ollie encourages a big breakfast, biscuits, fried salt pork and all the coffee that a man could want. For Ollie a big breakfast is just that. After taking minimum rations for days he makes up for his losses. Finally full, he organizes the work for the camp. First, the mules. Each animal is taken to the stream, washed down, hoofs inspected, groomed and returned to their side in the tall grass. Every member of the caravan takes part in the mule bathing, mainly because Ollie demands the participation. As a result not only do the mules get bathed but everything within one hundred feet of the stream gets the same bath as the night before. The stream is flowing almost pure white for several hours.

After the bath, the wagons are cleaned, hubs greased, axles inspected and all of the leather gear oiled down. By mid-afternoon a small crowd has gathered just out of ear shot and watches the activity. It's impossible to tell if the crowd is watching the activity or if they have never seen giants before, could be a bit of both.

Just at supper time a small group of four boys bring into camp two big bags of catfish from Utah Lake. The elder statesmen of the group, "If you can get knee deep in the water, the mosquitoes don't bother ya." After some serious negotiations Ollie buys the fish. Other small groups bring home canned beans, tomatoes, corn and peaches. Ollie gladly buys the goods. Supper consists of fresh fish, beans, biscuits, canned peaches and sun tea, pure heaven.

One of the older men, Elder Brice, approaches Ollie, "I see you have a lot of younger men with you."

"They are all my sons."

Elder Brice raises his eyebrows and with a slight grin looks up at Ollie, "Be aware that there are heathens about. Just north of here is an evil place, Gold Town."

"We will avoid the town and the inhabitants. Thank you, Elder Brice."

The mood around the camp fire is of quiet satisfaction, each man knowing what has been accomplished and knowing they have the will to do it again. Tomorrow is the day to finish the trek. Salt Lake City.

Chapter Twenty-Three

Ocher and Gordon are seated side by side again as the sun comes up. The wagons will be at Orem's trading post by noon.

"You're awful quiet, Gordon. How come?"

"You ain't going back with us, are you?"

"No, I'm not."

"What you gonna do next, Uncle Ocher?"

"I'm meeting a friend here and we'll be heading into the mountains for the summer."

"I wish you was going back with us."

"Were going back," Ocher corrects.

"Oh yeah, were going back."

"I appreciate that, but I want to see what's out there. As soon as my friend gets here and we get outfitted, I'll be headin' out. Don't worry, Ollie will know how to find me if need be." Gordon hesitates and finally reaches around Ocher and hugs him. Gordon doesn't say a word the rest of the way into Salt Lake.

A small man with a too-long great-coat is standing on the porch of Oren's Trading Post when the wagons start arriving in town. The full untrimmed beard does nothing to increase his stature, especially when Ollie steps down and shakes the man's hand. "The boys weren't lying when they said they had been trading with giants. If you'll pull the wagons around back, we can start unloading straight away. I'm Ezekiel Oren." He turns and walks back into the store.

At the rear loading dock Ollie takes charge of the unloading. A small crowd of children and a few older men have gathered to point and talk about the freight being unloaded from the wagons. Bolts of cloth, shovels, barrels of flour, rice, sorghum, seeds, buttons, shoes, hard candy, and string for candles are just a few of the items observed. Mr. Orem and Ollie tally each item as it's unloaded. After the count is agreed on, the freight is moved into the storage area of the store. There's no nonsense about Mr. Orem, just straight faced business. He does surprise the men when lunch is delivered to the dock, but insists that the meal is eaten in shifts and only after a rather lengthy prayer.

When the last of the goods is set on the loading dock and checked off the bill of lading, Mr. Oren turns to Ollie, "The tally is correct. You and your men are to be commended. If you'll join me in my office, we can conclude our business."

During the afternoon, a large pot of coffee is started and the entire crew, except Ollie, gathers around the fire to wait for his return. The pride and exhaustion is evident on each face. There are no longer any boys in the group and each man knows they have shared an adventure that will be told around other camp fires, over bunk house meals and with others who have been lucky enough to have lived through such an undertaking. The fact that half of the journey still lies ahead doesn't dampen the triumphant atmosphere around the coffee pot.

Ollie steps out of the shadow of the storage area with what appears to be a side of beef slung over his shoulder. Mr. Orem is just behind him struggling with a wooden box filled to the brim with, based on the aroma, fresh baked goods. Three men of the wagon train wrestle the beef into the nearest wagon. "See that notch in the mountains? We'll make camp there and cook up some beef. There are some bags of corn still on the cob sitting just inside the storeroom. Gordon, fetch them will ya? We'll cook some up for us and share some with the mules. They deserve a treat as well."

Chapter Twenty-Four

A breeze is moving through the cottonwood grove carrying the aroma of beef roasting. The men have divided up into groups around the different roasting fires waiting to attack the beef and fixings. The mules, munching corn on the cob, are bivouacked across and downstream of the camp.

Ollie is finally relaxed, sitting against a log with a cup of hot coffee. "Ocher, when we get down to the trading post, I'm gonna give the boys two dollars of their wages so they can fill up their kit and splurge a little. I'll give you yours now or in the morning. I expect you'll be finding your friend and heading out pretty quick."

"I'd rather have my wagon and five mules than money. The wagon I can sell and the mules we can use."

Ollie takes a sip of coffee. "Deal, that's five mules we don't have to carry water for. We don't have enough freight to fill all the wagons going back anyway, just some furs, timber and barrels of salt leaving plenty of room for extra water barrels. We'll be taking a bit more vittles as well. Jerky gets a might tiresome."

"Ollie, I do need one favor. Take the horse with you. I sure don't want to be called a horse thief, especially that old thing. When you heading out?"

"Today is Friday. We'll head back to town tomorrow, load the wagons and camp the same place down south of town then head out on Monday."

Ocher stands, tossing the dregs out of his coffee cup. "I'll help load up supplies and fill my own kit. After that I'm going to scout around a bit but I'll see you off on Monday. Probably camp there for a day or so, watch your back trail, just in case. You are carrying some money with you. Word gets around."

"Thanks, Ocher. I know Marta and some of the boys will miss you." The big man smiles. "Aw hell, so will I."

Somewhere in the camp the call comes, "Supper."

Chapter Twenty-Five

Ollie decides to wait until the caravan gets to the store before handing out wages. "I want them boys to mind their business, not dream about store bought goods."

For the most part, this is the first pay day for most of the younger "teamsters" and two dollars is a lot of money. The mules are hitched, a quick meal and coffee all completed well before dawn.

The wagons all move out of the grove and into town, gathering behind the store. Mr. Oren has each parcel brought out to the loading dock and placed on a scale to be weighed. Ollie has drawn little rectangles representing wagons on a piece of paper.

"Packet one of firs weighs twenty two pounds," Mr. Orem announces.

Ollie would repeat the weight and note the weight next to one of the rectangles. "Put that one in Jeremy's wagon." When the total weight reaches Ollie's predetermine limit, "Move the wagon over into the shade."

"That's the last of it, Mr. Van Derr. Here's your bill of lading," Mr. Oren announces. He leans in and whispers something to Ollie.

"We appreciate that," Ollie whispers back.

Ollie announces. "You've got two hours to look about. Meet me around front and I'll give each of you two dollars against your wages."

The boys stand about for a moment, finally realizing what Papa O has just said.

"Two dollars! I'm gonna buy ..." the calm erupts. Ollie's bulk saves him from the stampede.

The younger members of the crew rush into the store. The more mature members rush a little slower. The fact that there are a lot more goods to buy in San Francisco doesn't mean much. This is Salt Lake stuff.

The first fifty cents is invested in nothing anybody really needs. Candy (chocolate), candy (peppermint) and some other candy.

Oren's store has a big deep basement with ice piled high and covered with hay and burlap. "Boys, Mr. Oren has a treat for us. He has put some bottles of sassafras on ice for us. Jorge and Jeremy are bringing them up now," Ollie announces.

Jorge hands out the cold bottles each one dripping with melting ice. The boys gather in several of the shady spots on the porch.

"That's mighty good and cold. Wish we could have some on the trail home," Gordon says, wiping off his mouth on the sleeve of his new checkered shirt.

Two men coming from the direction of Gold Town ride up the street, stopping in front of the store. Before stepping out of the saddle, the bigger of the two pushes his wide brim hat back from his forehead. "Well lookey here. You boys afraid to have a real drink?" He steps down and walks up to Gordon who is sitting in the middle of the front porch with another boy on each side. The big man starts to reach for the bottle in Gordon's hand.

The front porch of the store is wider than most porches and the two men don't see who is sitting in the shadows. "I wouldn't do that if I was you," Ocher says in a low pleasant voice. "These are my brothers and I wouldn't take kindly to you disturbing any of them. Be glad to get you your own bottle, but don't go touching the boy's drink."

The red headed man is well over six feet and built powerful enough to intimidate most men. "Me drink sassafras? Mister that's an insult. Why don't you step off that porch before I come up there and drag you into the street?"

Before Ocher can stand up, Ollie and Jorge step out of the shadow of the porch.

Jeremy emerges holding two unopened bottles. "Sure you won't join us?"

The two men stare in stunned silence at the giants standing before them. The smaller of the two men says. "I'd just as soon have that sassafras, much obliged." The bigger man also takes a bottle, his eyes shifting between Ollie and Jorge.

Ocher leans forward in his chair, "Gordon, you and the other boys move off the step and let these cowboys go on about their business."

On the way into the store, both men stop where Ocher is standing in the shade. The red head turns toward Ocher. "This ain't over. They won't always be around to protect you," pointing his bottle toward the three seven footers.

The front porch respite continues without further interruptions. When the two cowboys leave toting their purchases they only glare at Ocher, but no words are exchanged. They saddle up and ride toward the direction of Gold Town.

"Well boys, time to get the wagons started. I'll meet you there," Ollie says walking toward the staging area.

Ocher leans against an upright porch post. *I really want to see what's out there, but I'm sure going to miss these guys.* Finally he steps off the porch and follows his brothers to the wagons.

The novelty of kids' spending money transitions into the routine of men inspecting the wagons and mules. The packages are stored and the chatter of "See what I bought?" is replaced by the jargon of professional teamsters, almost. A giggle or two still invades the serious tones. The driving teams have completed the walk arounds when Ollie arrives. He's carrying a large parcel wrapped in burlap. Without saying a word he places the bundle in his oversized wagon.

Mr. Orem is following Ollie with a second parcel. "Gentlemen, I wish you good luck for your return to San Francisco."

"Mr. Oren thanks for everything. If you're ever in San Francisco, come out to the house. You'd certainly be welcome."

"Thank you, Mr. Van Derr. That's a gracious offer."

"Ok, Honey Bee, enough lolly gagging. Let's be moving along." The usual grunts and groans from the mules is absent. As Ollie has said, "We'll be traveling light."

Ocher's wagon is empty and one of the other wagons is loaded with empty barrels. The rest have light loads, so the trip to the camp site is two hours shorter. The camp is organized, mules attended to and fire wood gathered for the night. Ollie hauls out the two large parcels and opens them. He unpacks fried chicken, potato salad, biscuits, jelly, butter, two kinds of pickles, milk and assorted pies. "I thought we should have a proper meal before we start out. Tomorrow we make ready, load the water barrels and we leave on Monday." Ollie's speech goes pretty much unheard as everybody is looking at the food.

Ocher does his share and more in preparing his family for the return trip. Although there's less livestock, there's been extra water barrels filled and loaded onto the wagons.

"We cut it a bit too close coming east, won't make that mistake going west," Ollie laments to anybody who will listen. Supper isn't as grand as the beef from the night before, but there's plenty for everybody. As the evening progresses each man realizes what the Monday will bring and the camp gets quieter by stages until there's no more talking at all. Without speaking, one by one each man not on watch retreats to his blanket.

Monday morning Ollie is up well before dawn getting the wagon train focused on the task at hand. There will be no long goodbyes or time to think or worry about the desert. The boys are focused on staying on task. Ollie does walk over to Ocher before stepping into his wagon. "Son, well I, well, uh, well." He finally just shakes hands almost dismembering Ocher's arm. "Time to go."

Ocher stands alongside the trail and nods and waves to each team as they drive off into the salt dust. It takes two teams passing him before he realizes something. Every member of the caravan is wearing the same checkered shirt, exactly the pattern as the one he is wearing.

As Jorge and Gordon pass by, "Had 'em made special. Had to, they don't come in big boys' sizes," Jorge yells.

Ocher is overwhelmed, "Thanks, boys."

He stands until he can no longer see Gordon waving.

Ocher steps up into his wagon and moves north to the highest point and as close to Gold Town to observe as much of the salt flats as he can. His wagon is loaded with enough supplies for ten days just in case he has to chase down anybody following the wagons. He sets up camp, gathers firewood, hobbles the mules, takes out his telescope and settles in to watch Ollie's back trail. He makes no attempt to hide his camp if someone is contemplating following. Maybe knowing he's watching will discourage any attempt.

By sunset of the first day, Ocher can still see the wagon train with the telescope. The tiny specks in the desert making a telltale dust cloud keep getting smaller. Ocher can see that Ollie is not going to stop the first night and by dawn he confirms it. The wagon train is no longer visible, not even a wisp of dust. He remains at his post for the rest of the day just to be sure. About an hour before sunset he moves his wagon to a more secure site and begins to set up for the night.

Ocher is sitting against the right rear wagon wheel when out of the night "Nobody followed your friends I see."

"Come on in, Ojos. I set up camp so even you could find me."

Chapter Twenty-Six

Ojos enters the camp. "This is much better than a lighthouse." He moves to the fire and notes that there's already a cup and a plate sitting next to the fire pit. He takes a sideways glance at Ocher.

Ocher just smiles. "I saw you yesterday stumbling through the brush and alarming the wildlife."

"At least you haven't forgotten how to look. I see that the big man still has to care for you. What will you do now that he is returning to the city?"

"That is a troubling question. For now I must wait until I meet your wife. She will teach me what I need to know, like she has taught you."

"My friend, you speak the truth. My wife and son are camped a days' walk southeast of here."

"I am looking forward to meeting your family. Before we leave I must return to the trading post." Ocher stands and retrieves several items from his wagon. "The new owner of the *Anne Belle* has sent you wages for your work on his ship." Ocher hands Ojos a snap purse that jingles when passed.

"I still have a gold coin left."

"Good. This is a gift from Mr. Stanley and me." Ocher hands Ojos the brand new Sharpe's rifle." You can buy more ammunition with the gold coin or with your wages. I don't know much about women but I would recommend you buy a real nice gift for your wife."

"White man speaks with great wisdom. I bring into camp a brand new rifle and present her with some beads or we will have a camp with no women in it."

"There are some things she would like at Orem's store. I'll help you decide," Ocher offers.

Ojos asks, "You do not plan on taking that wagon into the mountains, do you?"

"No, that's why I must return. I've already sold it to the man at the livery stable. I still own the mules. He'll buy them if we don't need all of them."

Ojos says, "I will think on it." He stands stretches and turns to Ocher. "There are some evil men in that town over there," pointing toward Gold Town. "I will take the first watch."

"Yeah, I've already met two of them."

Ojos grunts. "You seem to make friends wherever you go. Get some sleep."

Ojos is putting the makings together for skillet bread when Ocher returns from the stream with the coffee pot full of water. The rising sun hasn't quite decided on the morning colors. Ojos is kneading the dough mixture before flattening the balls into the skillet. There's a sizzle followed by the scent of the cooking bread. Bacon is hanging over a stick suspended above the fire dripping fat into the coals. Ocher drops a handful of coffee into the boiling water and sets out two cups.

Ojos looks over at Ocher. "We can get to my summer lodge much quicker if we all ride. Four riders and one pack animal. You will be in need of a rig. There is a herd of wild horses where we will summer. A saddle will come in handy."

It's well before noon when Ocher and Ojos arrive at the livery stable. The owner, good to his word, pays for the wagon. The mules are lead to a grass patch behind Orem's store and the two men walk around front.

"Morning, gentlemen," Mr. Orem nods to both men as they enter, never questioning Ojos's presence. The store is cool and dry, filled with the fragrances of candy, coffee, leather and odors that mix and mingle.

Ocher is standing at the counter when Ojos lays a large piece of leather, leather strips and a large needle on the counter. "What's that for?"

Before Ojos can answer the bell over the door rings and in walks the big red headed man and his trail partner.

The man is cautious at first but quickly realizes that Ollie or sons are not in the store. "You need to pick your company better, mule skinner. First it was a bunch of whelp pups and now a half-breed."

Ocher looks at the three silver dollars in his hand and without turning says, "I am particular about the company I keep. That's why you should leave."

The big cowboy isn't used to being sassed. "You've insulted me twice now. Most men don't get once."

Ocher, still with his back turned. "If you don't leave now, you'll also be shamed by a man without a gun."

"Why you little," he starts to say as he draws the pistol at his hip.

Ocher wheels around on his right heel. His right hand flicks so quick that it surprises everyone in the store, except Ojos who's sitting on a counter toward the back of the store eating a cracker. Two of the three silver dollars strike the big red-headed cowboy, one over the right eye, the second just below the nose. The impact is so unexpected that the man never draws his gun, he just reaches up to his face. His right eye is already swelling shut and his two front teeth have been loosened. The man's situation doesn't improve. Ocher is standing directly in front of him with a knife point just under his chin.

There's no help for the cowboy. The third silver dollar has struck his trail partner right between the eyes knocking him unconscious.

Ocher applies a little upward pressure to his knife, drawing blood. "Time to leave. Gather up your friend and get out. I could just as easily have killed you. Next time I will."

The big man, obviously shaken by the encounter, hefts his partner to his shoulder. He struggles under the weight. The unconscious man's feet knock can goods to the floor as they traverse the aisle. Ojos, being the gentlemen, holds the door open.

Ocher turns to Mr. Orem. "Sorry about that. I hope that doesn't hurt your business."

"Not at all. They have stores in Gold Town. I don't cheat the men as they do but I would rather trade with my own people. Could I trade you for those silver dollars? Never seen anything like that before."

"Sure, Mr. Oren."

"Just to be safe, you should take your goods through the back. I wish you luck. You are both welcome back anytime."

Ocher and Ojos tote their supplies through the storeroom and onto the loading dock of the store. "We're fortunate that Ollie knows his mules," Ojos remarks as he ties down a load. "These are good size mules, that saddle you have will fit. With a smaller mule the saddle will slip and you'd be riding under the mule. You do know how to ride a horse don't you?"

"Rode a lot of burros, can't be much different, except for the saddle. I'll manage." Ocher steps up into his saddle. Ojos settles a saddle blanket on his mule and throws a leg over, grabs the lead for a pack mule, and heels the mule into motion. The trailing mules just fall into line.

Ojos leads the procession northeast to present a false trail. Around noon they head south and then east. "I do not wish those men to follow, so we will take extra time before going to where my family is camped."

"What am I supposed to do with that leather?"

"Learn a lesson."

"Oh."

Ojos rides out of talking distance.

Sure is different from the jungle, but when you get right down to it, it's the same. The jungle is surrounded by water you can't drink. Here it's bigger islands with trees and brush surrounded by sand or dirt. Either way you have to have fresh water, Ocher muses. Yep, water is the key to it all, fresh clean water.

Nightfall finds the men camped miles from any civilization and above the eight thousand foot mark. The thin air is new to Ocher. "The air is mighty clean smelling up here, but don't seem to be enough of it." The highest peak he has experienced in the Philippine jungle is a couple of hundred feet.

"Very clean. No smell of civilization," Ojos responds smiling at Ocher. "Rest if you like. I come back before the snow comes and find you."

"Ok, just leave me a mule. I might get hungry."

"Mule no good. Bear eat you and leave mule alone."

"I've never seen a bear, heard talk about them. Never seen one."

"Bear always see you first. When you hear growl, be too late. Get close up look. Breath the same. You get used to clean air."

The sun is beginning to set behind the tallest of the peaks when Ojos picks an overnight camp. They quickly set about organizing the camp and by dusk, beans and beef are cooking and the coffee boiling. The mules have been picketed and fed.

"Tomorrow before noon we will meet with my family," Ojos remarks over supper. "They are camped in the foot hills of the Uintahs. I am anxious to be with them again. Do you think those men are following?"

Ocher sets his plate aside. "I don't think so. But I think they might work up the courage to try later on. The more ground we can put behind us the better." Ojos, with his usual guttural grunt, "I agree."

"The mules can stand watch tonight," Ocher says. Ojos again grunts in approval.

Chapter Twenty-Seven

Ojos slows the pace. Since leaving their overnight camp, they've climbed to over ten thousand feet.

"Appears that the mules don't appreciate all this fresh clean air," Ocher says in between breaths."

"I see that maybe you take up too much of the air, my friend. Leave some for the mules.

"I think maybe you bought too many things at the trading post and have loaded them too heavy.

"We rest the mules soon."

Ojos brings the group to a halt just inside the shadows of a tree line. Ahead of them is a valley of lush green grass with a stream running along the west side. Ojos steps down from his mule and squats with his hands hanging loosely between his knees. "Be still my friend."

Ocher stays perfectly still in the saddle. He strokes the mule to keep the mule calm and quiet. Nothing seems to move. There's no sound. Finally the forest seems to breathe and the sounds of birds, squirrels and other wildlife fill the air. Ojos remains still. Then across the meadow a small head covered in jet black hair pops up and drops down just as quick. Ocher is surprised at the movement but remains still. Again the head pops up several yards to left of the original reveal and stays up just a tick more. Then the meadow erupts from the last location of the head. A small boy stampedes out of the grass toward Ojos. Ocher cannot understand the words but there's no doubt of the meaning.

"Papa!" yells Ojos's son.

The son rushes up the hill to his father. Ojos remains crouched until the boy flings himself into his father's arms. The boy looks at Ocher and the mules but his enthusiasm is focused on his father. He gestures and speaks excitedly apparently about what's happened in Ojos' absence. Finally he runs out of steam. Ojos places the boy on the ground beside him. "Ocher, this is my son Slow To Walk." He turns to the boy. "You must speak to Mr. Ocher in English until he learns our words."

The boy immediately regains his head of steam. "Mr. Ocher, you swam in the big water with my father? You know a giant? You fish with a rock? You sleep on a platform? What is a jungle? Where is your gun."

Ojos places his hand on the young man's shoulder. "There will be time for stories later. We must leave this place and move to the high mountains." Slow To Walk looks at his father and in an instant is running down through the meadow. Ocher leads his mule out of the timber line following the boy's trail.

The camp is compact but efficient, located within a tumble of rocks. The cooking fire is small, smokeless, set back in a hollow that reflects heat into the sleeping area. A small woman with jet black hair, braided pony tails, dressed in tanned hides and barefoot, is cooking over a pot next to the fire.

"You are late," she says with a smile, "I thought I might have to find a better husband."

Ojos, also smiling, "I went around the world looking for a better wife, I could not find one. This is my friend Ocher. Ocher, this is Water That Sparkles Over The Stones In The Morning Light." She looks at Ocher, "I am called Water Woman. Thank you for keeping my husband from trouble, again."

"He takes a lot of watching," Ocher responds.

"There is food," she says and points to the pot. "You eat and I will make ready to leave." She looks past Ocher and sees the mules. "We all ride?"

Ojos just grunts his yes grunt.

Slow To Walk, under the direction of Water Woman, makes ready to move. The camp site all but disappears.

"It will rain soon. This camp will not be found," Ojos says as he looks around the site. "Ocher, you see that notch between those hills?"

"Yes."

"You follow, check no one is behind us. We meet there when rain starts. Let mules rest a bit before you leave. You get lost Slow To Walk will find you." Ojos starts to say something else when Water Woman hisses at him. Ojos looks down at the ground then looks over at Ocher, "She thinks I disrespect you. I do not."

As Ojos has predicted, by mid-afternoon a thunderstorm moves in. Ocher has heard thunder storms before but not like this. The thunder seems to come from many directions. He realizes quickly that it is just a thunder event that echoes through the hills and mountains. The mules flinch as each thunder booms resounds. Then the rain, monsoon type rain. Ocher is concerned that this rain, like he is used to, doesn't go on for days and weeks as it would in the jungle. Slow To Walk is standing under a rock outcropping and points in the direction he wants Ocher to go. The rain is so loud any conversation would be impossible.

Ojos is sheltered in the lee of a rock face with Water Woman and the mules. They are wet but not as wet as Ocher.

"We will have a cold camp here until the rain stops. When the moon rises we will move on. Tomorrow it will rain again, soon no one can follow."

Water Woman hands Ocher a blanket, "Your clothes will dry faster if you take them off." She looks down at his cowboy boots. "My husband tells me you bought leather at the store."

"Yes."

"Good, I will teach you to make proper shoes."

At the full moon, the rain has stopped. The caravan continues up and into the mountains. A little after sunrise Ojos stops the procession. "We will camp for a while. From here we can go in many directions. If we are followed they must come through this pass and we will know of them. Wife, we are hungry. Prepare a warm meal, then we will rest."

Slow To Walk helps hang Ocher's wet clothes on some low hanging branches. "Mr. Ocher, where is your mother and father?"

The hiss from Water Women is immediate.

"That's ok, Water Woman. Slow To Walk, my mother and father died when I was very young. I don't remember them."

Slow To Walk hesitates before continuing, "That is sad, but you are here now. We will be happy."

The camp is quickly organized, a fire started and a quick meal prepared. Ocher, wrapped in his blanket and barefoot, goes back down the trail to watch. Slow To Walk brings two bowls of stew and joins the watch. He remains silent although Ocher can sense that the boy has many more questions.

Throughout the day clouds gather from the west. By midafternoon another rain storm is approaching. Ojos calls, "It is time." The small group is more than a mile away from the resting camp when the rain begins and covers their trail. By nightfall they have arrived at the Ojos's campsite. In the fading light all Ocher can see is a lake and a large shadow he assumes is a mountain on the opposite of the water. Ojos slides from the mule, "This is a good place. You will see it better tomorrow and then we will choose the best location."

By the time the moon comes up, the wet clothes have been dried and supper has been eaten. The mules have been temporarily hobbled, wood gathered and beds made. Ojos is confident that they have not been followed so no guard is posted. As the fire burns down to coals the camp is quiet and warm under the stars.

When Ocher sits up and his blanket falls he is awestruck at his surroundings. What he thought was a lake is actually two lakes nestled at the east facing the base of a granite mountain rising well over eleven thousand feet. Huge boulders of granite that have broken off of the mountain are strewn across the opposite side of the lake and sparkle in the rising sun. A strip of land cuts between the two lakes creating a spillway. The only way to the opposite shore is to walk around the shoreline of either lake. About one hundred yards from the overnight camp is a grove of Aspen with large boulders mixed into the trees. There's a meadow below the trees with a small stream meandering through it. Ojos has already released the mules and they've taken up residence in the grassy meadow.

"We'll make our camp in the grove. We can defend ourselves from there but we can also escape," Ojos remarks as he walks back to camp carrying the picket strings used to hobble the mules.

Ocher, Ojos and Slow To Walk take their directions from Water Woman. She knows exactly how she wants the camp set up. "Put the fire wood there so I do not have to hunt for it." The cooking fire is placed in one of the many natural niches weathered out in the boulders. The cooking fire looks like a natural oven with chimney when it finally passes her inspection.

"I will place the sleeping place there and cut aspens to cover them," says Ojos moving away from camp, anxious to use his new store bought hatchet.

Water Woman nods her approval. "I will place my new mirror and combs there." She points toward a ledge on the rock.

By sunset the camp can rival any hotel with the exception of having no doors or windows. "Slow To Walk, would you like to go catch some fish for supper?" Water Woman asks.

No need for an answer. He is already sprinting toward the lake.

Supper is fresh trout with wild onions, dandelions, and squaw grass.

Chapter Twenty-Eight

Ocher sits watching the herd of wild horses in the meadow below. He has set up his own camp two miles or so from the main camp. Ojos, Slow To Walk and he tracked the herd of wild horses to this valley. That was a week ago. Each day when the herd comes to graze Ocher has moved closer and closer to them. The first day the stallion pinto raises the alarm and the herd stampedes out of the meadow back into the foot hills. Now the pinto just watches Ocher as Ocher watches him.

On the first day alone with the herd, Ocher sits on the only rock in the meadow. He is sewing, or attempting to sew, his leather into moccasins. Every time Water Woman shows him how to make the moccasins it looks so easy. So far his attempts have resulted in being barefoot in about two strides.

Ocher faces the herd but ignores them for the most part. The pinto seems intrigued by the activity, sniffs the air, paws the ground and eventually moves closer and closer. Ocher continues his work until the pinto is within one hundred feet. Ocher continues to sew but also begins to speak in a soft even voice to the horse. "Curious aren't you?" The pinto's ears prick up and the horse takes a challenging position when he hears the man speak. Curiosity overtakes his fears and as he accepts the talking.   When a mare knickers from the herd and the spell is broken, the pinto turns, kicks up his heels and returns to the herd. That is how it begins.

A week goes by and each day the pinto inches closer and closer to the man. Ocher has already sewn two pair of moccasins but continues the same activity trying to let the curious horse get close enough to touch. When the pinto does approach touching distance, Ocher turns his back on the stallion hiding the leather work. The move just increases the curiosity of the pinto. Finally Ocher holds out the moccasin, the pinto leans in, sniffs, pulls back slightly then sniffs of Ocher. "What do you think boy, we gonna be friends?" By now the pinto is used to the man's voice. The inspection completed, the horse turns and without looking back struts to his herd.

By the end of the second week, the pinto is grazing next to Ocher's sitting rock. "Well fella, I have to leave in the morning. I'm out of, well everything, but mostly coffee. It'll be just a couple of days. If Slow To Walk hasn't eaten all of the hard candy, I'll bring you a taste." Ocher slides off the rock, stretches and starts walking to his camp. The pinto follows for about two hundred feet, stops to watch Ocher for a time then finally turns and wanders across the meadow to the herd.

Chapter Twenty-Nine

The morning dawns bright and beautiful. Ocher doesn't want to leave the meadow and the pinto but he has been away from the main camp for two weeks. He's out of supplies and misses the company of Ojos, Water Woman and especially Slow To Walk. He leaves enough of the temporary camp intact so the pinto can remember his scent and so he doesn't have to start all over establishing a new camp. He hefts his pack and starts back toward the lakes. It would be easier with a mule but Ojos points out that the mule will distract the herd, so Ocher is afoot.

At about noon, he stops just for a rest and to eat the last of the jerky and grab a drink of water. No use to start a fire. There's nothing to heat and it's warm enough so no fire is needed. He's at the foot of the lakes when he hears a sharp pistol shot coming from the direction of the camp. Knowing that the only gun in camp is Ojos's rifle and the sound now echoing off the granite mountain isn't a rifle report, he drops his pack and starts to run toward camp. Ocher hasn't gone a hundred feet when he hears the sound of a large animal barreling through the woods toward him. *I hope that ain't a bear.*

The pinto breaks through the brush and rushes toward Ocher, coming to a stop just ahead of him. The pinto turns and looks at Ocher as if to say, *we can get there quicker if you ride, now get aboard.* Ocher jumps astride the pinto and grabs a handful of mane and the horse is quickly at the gallop. Ocher adapts to the bareback riding just enough to see over the pinto's head into the camp.

There are two men and two horses. One man is astride a horse pointing a hand gun at Water Woman. She is huddled over Ojos. Ojos appears to be holding his arm. The second man is on foot trying to chase down Slow To Walk.

Ocher recognizes the immediate threat is the man with the gun. The pinto apparently has come to the same conclusion and heads straight toward the rider.

Slow To Walk is leading the second man away from the melee toward the trees.

Water Woman is brandishing one of her brand new hunting knives and is being quite vocal. Ocher can't understand her but can guess about her topic.

Too late the man on the horse turns to see Ocher coming straight at him. He starts to turn and level the gun at Ocher. Without warning, the pinto changes course to the right, just as an amazing sight takes place. The man on the horse soars backward. The horse continues forward passing Ocher and the pinto. A clap of what sounds like thunder follows.

The cowboy chasing Slow To Walk stops at the sound of thunder and rushes back toward Water Woman and Ojos with his gun drawn.

Slow To Walk disappears into the tree line.

The pinto races toward a point in between Water Woman and the approaching gunman.

The gunman changes his focus from Water Woman to the approaching pinto and brings his hand gun to bear on Ocher.

The pinto slows and comes to a stop, blocking the advance toward Water Woman and Ojos.

Ocher leaps off the pinto, lands on his feet, and rolls forward while reaching for the knife between his shoulder blades. As soon as he regains his footing, he throws the knife at the gunman hitting him squarely in the chest. Both men are down.

Water Women is gesturing toward the location Slow To Walk escaped into the trees and is saying something that Ocher can't understand.

Ocher's concern is what he thinks is a lightning strike followed by thunder. But there's not a cloud in the sky. Then he remembers hearing a similar sound just before he and Ojos went over the side of the *Anne Belle*. A gun shot.

Ojos is sitting up, still holding his arm. There is blood seeping between his fingers. He points in the same direction as Water Women with the hand of his injured arm.

Ocher races to the cowboy and retrieves his knife and starts toward the trees to protect Slow To Walk from whoever is out there shooting. No need.

An older man dressed in well-worn deer skins steps out of the aspen trees with a rifle slung over his shoulder, holding Slow To Walk by the hand. The pair starts walking toward the camp. Ocher immediately recognizes the man, Abel Jones.

Ocher smiles and shakes his head. He turns and walks over to see if Water Woman needs any help with Ojos.

"I'm ok, or will be when my wife quits hurting me. Who is that holding my son captive?"

"That is Abel Jones, the man I met in the desert. He is not holding Slow To Walk captive. It's probably the other way around."

"You will live, my husband, for a while anyway."

Ocher proceeds to see who the attackers were. He recognizes both men. These are the men from Orem's Store.

Slow To Walk detaches his hand from Abel and sprints into his mother's arms.

"You were brave, my son. Who is your friend?"

"He is called Abel. He is a mountain man."

Abel follows Slow To Walk into camp,

"Ocher."

"Abel."

"This must be Ojos."

"Yep and this Water That Sparkles Over The Stones in the Morning and you've already met Slow To Walk."

"I am called Water Woman."

"Howdy folks," Abel looks around the scene. "Don't mean to give advice when not asked for, but might want to consider moving from here. Didn't see no other flatlanders but never can tell."

"You are wise, Mr. Abel Jones. This is a place of death. We will move."

"Call me Abel. Can't get far today. Tell you what, if it ain't putting you out much. If you'll get supper on, I'll clean up the vermin."

Ocher and Abel gather up the horses and tie the cowboys down across the saddles. The pinto watches from outside the camp but makes no move to participate. He and Slow To Walk are standing nose to nose.

"We'll bury those two and hide their saddles and gear. Don't want to be riding around on gear someone might recognize. Might bring more trouble. The horses we'll just let go. Same reason."

When Ocher and Abel return to camp Ojos is packing, Water Woman is busy with cooking and directing Ojos. Slow To Walk and the pinto are down by the lake fishing.

Water Woman pours coffee into a cup and hands it to Abel. Ocher hands him a jar of honey.

Ojos, trying to restore order from all of the confusion, offers his hand to Abel, "Welcome to our fires. You have friends here, always."

Abel tips his hat, "Much obliged."

Over super of deer steaks and wild onions Ocher asks, "Abel, how'd you get to be here?"

In the tradition of tall tales Abel begins. "Well it all began when I met up with some lads north of Salt Lake that said they met a giant. The boys went on to say that a smaller man with them played hob with two bad men using just silver dollars. Most of that type don't care for being bested. Figured they might hunt you down. It's a tough chore hiding a trail with that many mules. So's I found me a place to cozy in and waited. Sure enough, here they came. Followed 'em up here. Early this morning thought I'd try and get ahead of 'em and find you. They beat me to it, them riding and me walking. Well you know the rest."

"I bet that story will get better every time you tell it," offers Ocher.

Abel just laughs, "Probably."

Ojos belches loudly, "Tomorrow we leave. It will be your burden to teach that one," pointing his chin toward Ocher.

"Where will you go, Ojos?"

"Better you not know, my friend. There may be others better than the ones that came."

"He's right, Ocher. Can't tell what you don't know," Abel remarks.

"Mr. Ocher, where will you go?" Slow To Walk asks.

Ocher is quiet for quite a while, finally, "I don't really know. Seems I bring grief on my friends wherever I go."

"You did not bring these men to our camp," Water Woman says. "That burden is not upon you. It is upon them."

"She's right," Abel says.

"She is a wise woman Ocher," Ojos responds. "Evil men like those seek out decency to destroy it. They can't carry the burden of goodness in their hearts. It is a sickness that has no cure. That is not your burden."

"Speaking of evil. Came across what was left of that captain fella. Rode his horse to death and the desert...did the rest. No need for details."

"Does the pinto go with you, Mr. Ocher?" Slow To Walk asks, breaking the somber mood.

"That's pretty much up to him," Ocher answers.

"Ocher, I'm heading south of here to a place I call The Sands of Many Colors. It ain't as green as here, but it's beautiful in its own way. You're welcome to come along. Besides Ojos has tasked me with trying to teach you something. Could burden me some but if you're willin'."

"Isn't that down around the Apache Nation?"

"Yep, scared?"

"I reckon I best go with you just in case you wander into those folks."

Chapter Thirty

Water Woman wakes the camp early. There's no lingering over coffee or storytelling. When the grey dawn gives way to full sunlight the camp has been well disguised. The only real evidence is the fire and smoke ash of Water Woman's cook fire.

The mules sense what is happening and have wandered into the camp, the pinto leading his new herd. Ocher decides to saddle his riding mule instead of trying the pinto. The pinto watches the procedure and when the saddle is cinched in place, he struts over, sniffs the rig and backs away.

Ojos walks over to Abel and Ocher who are just finishing packing their mules. "Go safe. You know of the Apaches. There is much hate within them." He stands for a second, sealing the conversation with an ever-present grunt, turns and follows his family as they disappear into the trees.

Ocher is still watching after Ojos when Abel breaks into his thoughts. "They say there's no word in the Crow language for goodbye. Don't know if I believe that or not, cause I've never heard it. That's their way. Don't let it bother you none. We best be moving. Time to see if that pinto wants to come along."

Ocher turns in his saddle at the foot of the lake. Ojos, Water Women and Slow To Walk are standing at the edge of the tree line. They wave.

"Ain't never seen that before. They must think highly of you for such an outward demonstration. That's a big show of respect."

The night is quiet and a bit lonely with the ever-present energy of Slow To Walk missing. Ocher is experiencing feelings that he never even considered: missing someone. Marta, Ollie, the boys and now Ojos, Water Woman and Slow To Walk. They have all taken a part of him with them as they leave. As a boy, his entire focus was to leave his jungle *family*. He was glad to leave and leave nothing behind, but now.

"I can see something been vexing you, Ocher? I got good ears."

Ocher instincts had told him to trust this man when they first met. Nothing has changed, "When I left where I was raised I never felt regret or any thought about returning. It filled my heart with joy, as Water Woman would say. It ain't the same now."

"I think I understand. Go on."

"When I left Marta and then Ollie and his family, my heart certainly wasn't filled with joy, quite the opposite."

"Those people saw there was no evil in your heart. If they had seen it ,they wouldn't have allowed you into their family circle. But they did."

"But I exposed them to my past."

"Everybody has a past, especially out here in the west. Even me. Don't let your past guide your future. That's my mistake."

"Mistake?"

"We aren't as different as you might think, Ocher. I chose to live a solitary life for basically the same reason that's now burdening you. Hate to admit it but I took the coward's way out. Don't allow anyone close so you don't have to worry about anyone."

"You have friends."

"No, I have encounters with people. I was never really inflicted with missing someone, a decision I made a long time ago. You're different. Your concern isn't for yourself but for those around you. You have a choice to make."

"But..."

"Leave it for now. One thing about traveling out here, you have time to cogitate over things."

"Thanks."

"Don't cotton to riding out of here but it's best we get down to the flat lands and Meeker's trading post on the quick step. I'll ride that far, but no further," Abel announces as he walks to his bedroll.

"All right, we can sell the extra mules when we get there and fill out our kit," Ocher responds as he heads to his own bedroll.

Just after sunrise Abel gives one last glance around the camp site to insure that they leave no glaring evidence of their existence. "If anyone is following us and they're trail wise, they will find this spot." He steps aboard his mule. With a slight nudge they start out of the mountains.

Abel is in the lead with his pack mule, Ocher a little behind with his pack mule and the pinto and his new herd following. It takes less than a mile for the pinto to decide his rightful place is not following but leading. He struts past Abel, snorts and takes the lead. When his mule herd tries to follow him to the front, he quickly educates them with a nip or two that they are designated to following not leading. The pinto also decides when and where they stop at noon and the first night's camp.

The only remark is from Abel, "Couldn't have picked a better place my own self."

After supper of venison jerky and coffee, Abel stands and rubs his left haunch, "Ain't used to sitting and riding. Be glad to be walking again."

"Can you make it to Meeker's or should we rig up a travois? Three or four days could be tough going." Ocher smiles as he takes a drink from his canteen.

"We'll just have to see about that, young 'un. You take a bit of advice from an old timer?"

Ocher smiles a crooked smile, "Yeah, if I knew one worth his salt."

"Good enough." Abel just shakes his head, "From all accounts, you're pretty handy in close. Out here, close is sometimes too late. You might consider a long gun."

"That's good advice, Abel, but I just don't feel the need."

"Not to put too fine an edge to it, but I wouldn't have been much help to you back yonder without this here old buffalo gun. At least give it some thought."

"You're right. I'm not saying I'll get me one, but I would take it kindly if you'd teach me shoot one. Deal?"

"You got yourself a deal."

Chapter Thirty-One

The next morning the pinto decides that it's time to be saddled. He stands like a prince being attended to, head held high, ears erect and looking down on his subjects until the saddle blanket hits his back. The strain to remain regal is an all-out effort. He endures the bit, saddle blanket, then the saddle. Just to establish who's in charge, when Ocher steps up into the saddle, the pinto walks casually to a tree and under a low branch as if to say, *You're up there because I allow it.* The order of march has been established. The pinto with Ocher allowed the honor of riding leads out. When someone or something makes an attempt to change the established order of things, the pinto makes a subtle reminder by rubbing up against a tree or just plain stopping until all is right.

Day by day the partnership between horse and rider deepens. The pinto seems to understand that they're a team and not competing for supremacy. When they all ride into Meeker, even the mules understand the hierarchy.

Meeker's isn't much: a saloon dry goods store in one building, a coral with a barn, and two falling down houses. The pinto stops short of town and Abel rides up beside, "Let's get our supplies and ride on. I'd soon be shuck of this place as quick as can be." Ocher just nods in agreement.

They ride in and stop at the stable. "Ocher, I'll see to our kit. You do the mule trading."

A rail thin man with arms that extend far beyond the cuffs of a tattered shirt steps out from the shadow of the barn, wipes his hands on a handkerchief he takes from the front pocket of his overalls. "Want to sell them mules? A man can always use a good mule. Mind if I look them over? "

"Go ahead. Might want to stay clear of the pinto. He ain't house broke."

The gaunt man seems to know what he's about and after a brief barter they come to a price. "Let's walk up to the store. We'll settle up. You just gonna leave that horse loose?"

"You want to try and hobble him?"

"Nope."

Ocher follows the man. The pinto, after helping himself to a drink, is standing in the shade of the barn with the pack mule.

The store smells pretty much like the barn and is only slightly cleaner. Abel has amassed a pile of goods on the counter. The man from the barn rounds the end of the counter, picks up a small tally book and begins calculating the purchases.

"Looks like I owe you thirty-one dollars." Ocher checks the figures and nods his approval, the goods are gathered and Abel and Ocher walk to the barn. The load is packed with quick efficiency and they leave, headed due west until they are out of sight, then turn south toward the Colorado River.

The last three months have spoiled Ocher with fresh clean lake water, lush forest and meadows. The contrast to the surrounding high desert is stark: no water, no tall green forests and certainly no lush green meadows. The surrounding vegetation is sparse, dry and brown. There are occasional clumps of pinions and cedars but not many. Now that Abel is walking, Ocher has more time to take in the scenery, or lack of it.

The pinto, still in command, doesn't seem to notice the change of terrain. He apparently is king of all he surveys, trees or sand.

"See that break in the brush about a mile out?" Abel asks. "Just to the west side is a small spring. We'll supper there. You go on ahead and get a fire going. I'll be along as soon as I make sure of our back trail."

Ocher just nods and prompts the pinto toward the spring. When Abel arrives, the coffee is boiling and Ocher is rolling dough for pan bread. "Beans, bacon and fry bread. Got some canned peaches too. The honey is sitting by your cup."

"Sounds fitting enough. We'll eat here by the spring but move on up this arroyo so the critters can get in during the night." Abel says as he moves toward the coffee pot.

After eating, they scatter the embers of the fire and cover any remaining evidence of the camp before moving away from the spring. The night is magnificent. Ocher has never seen so many stars before. In the high country camp, half of the sky was blocked by the mountain of the west side of the lake, but here there are no obstructions. It's well past midnight when he finally can sleep.

In the early grey dawn they are moving again but only a couple of miles south to another small spring. Abel takes a box of cartridge shells out of his pack, "We'll practice your shooting each morning then move on. The noise will attract, well everything. When they come to investigate, we'll be gone."

For two weeks each morning they practice then move on in separate directions and gather up again in the evenings, eat and move away to a cold camp.

"The Apaches don't bother me none, I been around them since I came out here. Sides we're well east of them. It's the other two legged critters that put the bother on me," Abel often laments.

They keep away from towns or settlements moving south by south west to his Sand of Many Colors.

Two days after crossing the Colorado River they arrive. Ocher is speechless. In every direction there are low mountains, arroyos and valleys bursting with colors. There's no description possible. With each turn of the head, the slightest change of angle of the sun, or any movement results in a complete new vista of colors. Ocher and Abel just stand and try to take it in. Even the pinto seems to be impressed.

Abel breaks the spell, "Never get used to it, but we stood long enough. By now every Navajo within fifty miles knows we're here. Let's make our camp. By sunset we'll know for sure. One thing to remember with Indians, don't back up a step. Stand your ground or they'll think you weak. If they're going to kill you, at least go out strong."

"Not many choices for a camp out here. It's awful pretty but dry as can be. We have to camp where there's water." Abel knows exactly where the water is and they move to it. Supper is done and they are sitting around taking in the setting sun when the Navajo come in from all sides, noisy and all show. Both men just look up and continue to just sip their coffee and try to convey to the small hunting party that they are nothing more than a minor annoyance. The leader dismounts with as much flair as he can gather, and speaks to Abel. Abel replies in the same tongue and the warrior reacts as if slapped. "I told him he and his party ride like old women and to go away, we are having coffee."

The brave steps forward and back hands the coffee cup from Abel, then pulls a black obsidian flint knife from his belt and makes a menacing

move toward the old mountain man. Abel
doesn't budge, so the brave turns toward Ocher.

"Abel, tell this fellow that I like the knife. He
can either give it to me as a gift or I'll take it
from him."

Abel is amused at the statement and tells the
brave what Ocher has said.

The Navajo brave moves at Ocher with the
knife in his right hand ready to strike. "If that's
the way you want it," Ocher stands up. Before
the brave can react, Ocher using his right hand,
grabs the brave's right hand, the one holding the
knife. With his left hand Ocher strikes the
Indian's shoulder joint with the ball of his hand,
dislocating the shoulder. The pain is immediate.

The brave yells something and drops the
knife.

"He says that hurts."

Just to make his point, Ocher then sweeps
the brave's legs with his right foot. As the brave
falls, Ocher turns the arm just slightly adding
just a bit more pain to the humiliation. He bends
down and picks up his new knife. Ocher removes
his own knife from his right boot and replaces it
with his new knife. Looking down at the warrior
he says, "Thanks." He drops his own knife at the
feet of the Navajo brave and sits back down. He
picks up Abel's cup, pours coffee and hands it to
Abel. Ocher then draws himself some coffee.

Abel says nothing, just grins.

The small hunting party is stunned at the
proceedings. A couple of the braves try not to
smile, but have to work at it. Finally the man on
the ground rises, scoops up his new knife with

his left hand, strolls back to his horse with a lot less swagger. He falls trying to mount and finally rides off toward the south with the hunting party.

"That's Blue Sand. We're not good friends," Abel says.

In the predawn, over coffee, Abel asks, "Can you fix Blue Sand's shoulder?"

"Yep."

"Probably should go into the village just south of here and do that. As much as we don't cotton to each other, it ain't fittin' to have his family starve because he can't hunt. I get along with the rest of the tribe. Ok by you?"

"Yep."

The entire village turns out to meet the men as they arrive. Abel is well known and welcomed as a friend by all, except one. There's much storytelling, pomp, and ceremony, lasting until sunset. Abel finally tells Three Toe Bear, the Chief, that they're here to make Blue Sand's shoulder work.

"Don't make too much of this, my friend, or you'll end up with a bride. Don't say yes to anything."

Blue Sand is summoned and is asked if he wants his shoulder to work. He reluctantly agrees. Ocher steps behind Blue Sand, drapes his left arm over the shoulder to hold it steady, and with his right hand at the back of the shoulder, snaps the dislocated shoulder back into place. To Blue Sand's credit, he remains stoic with the pain. He slowly raises his arm and gives a spirited yell and walks away. He never turns and looks at Ocher.

Three Toe Bear speaks for several moments. Abel shakes his head and also speaks for several moments. After some back and forth, "Time to go, Ocher."

"Ok by me."

The pinto had to work hard to keep up with the escaping Abel.

"That was close. We both almost ended up with wives. That old coot tried to give us some of his older wives so he could get some new ones."

Over the next ten days, they wander through Abel's desert. Between Ojos, Water Woman and Abel, Ocher's knowledge of his new home land grows. With the help of the Pinto, he feels he can now survive and enjoy the experience.

With the fire burned down to coals and the sky filled with stars, Ocher and Abel spend their last night as trail partners. In the morning the pair will head into Durango to replenish supplies. Abel is heading into Mexico to visit with his good friend Tyler Gomez at his horse ranch.

At a suggestion from Abel, Ocher is heading toward Pine Springs, Texas. He intends to meet some friends of Abel's, the Sterling Brothers. "Them two boys are trying to raise cattle on a horse ranch. By now they'll be ready to sell and head back east," Abel said one night over venison steaks.

The next morning they enjoy one last cup together and watch the performance of colors on the sand as the sun rises. At mid- morning, they enter Durango, Colorado, a real town with hotels, places to sit and eat, stores, blacksmith shop and civilization.

Ocher enters Jim's blacksmith's shop, "Howdy, you Jim?"

"Yep."

"You up for a challenge?"

"Could be."

"Want to try and shoe that pinto?"

Jim walks out to the pinto, slowly. He offers the horse an apple and talks in a soft voice. Jim moves to the front right leg and carefully lifts it and taps on the hoof with the end of a folded pocket knife just to see a reaction. He walks back to Ocher. "I'll give it a try. No promise though. I got a wife and two boys. No need to widow her. Cost you five dollars for the shoeing and dollar for all the apples that I'll need."

"How about you keep the mule and we call it even."

Jim walks over to the mule for an inspection. He walks back. "Ok by me."

Out of the shadows of the stable, "Abel, you old coot, good to see ya. I thought Blue Sand would have your hide by now. Who's that with you?"

Abel smiles, "Ocher, they pay this buzzard to be the sheriff of this place. Don't rightly know if he's any good at it though. Calls himself O'Keefe. Don't know if that's his real name, probably not." The sheriff, a man of about six foot, tanned to the color of Abel's deer skins, walks out from the shadows and offers his hand to Abel. Ocher steps down from the pinto and also shakes the sheriff's hand.

"I know," the Sheriff says, "Just passing through, stopping for supplies."

"That's right Doug. I'll be gone afore sunset," Abel responds.

"How about you, Ocher? Staying awhile?"

"No, Sheriff. I'll be selling that mule, and hope to get my horse shod. I'll be filling my kit and heading out myself before sunset."

The Sheriff shakes his head, "Hard to get a good tall tale anymore. Everybody in too big a hurry."

Abel and the Sheriff walk toward Durango Dry Goods leaving Ocher to haggle with the livery owner over the mule. Ten minutes later Ocher enters the cool confines of the dry goods store. The Sheriff is sitting with his feet propped up on a potbellied stove working on what appears to be a jaw breaker.

Abel is just finishing his resupply. He turns toward Ocher, "One last bit of advice. It will soon be the rainy season in Texas, so get a good poncho." He picks up his packages and walks out the door. "Be seeing ya."

The Sheriff mumbles around a mouth full of candy, "He does that to me every time he leaves. Don't let it fret ya none. He's a good man to call a friend."

Ocher nods, afraid to speak, picks up his packages. The new poncho on top, he turns to the Sheriff, "Be seeing you," and steps out the door.

The Sheriff drops his feet to the floor, looks to the clerk, "Now there's two of a kind."

Coming Soon -

Ocher Jones Western Series -
Book Two

Ocher's Rain

Ocher is sheltered from the west Texas *rain* contemplating his strategy to remain anonymous when fate changes his course. Two shots ring out from the dreary darkness drawing Ocher and the Pinto into a new adventure. And then a girl named Stacey, who changes everything.

Contact information:

Mike Gipson

msguscg@gmail.com

www.ingramcontent.com/pod-product-compliance
Lightning Source LLC
Chambersburg PA
CBHW032141170626
46808CB00006B/2323